Readers love

An Unconventional Courtship

"This is probably one of the sweetest stories that I have read in a long time."

—Guilty Pleasures

"A win-win all around. Enjoy. I did."

—Literary Nymphs Reviews

Wings of Love

"…a heartfelt and very sweet romance that I couldn't put down once I started."

—Night Owl Reviews Top Pick

Treasure of Love

"I enjoyed a lot Dax and Jack's love dance, and I think Dax adopted the right strategy to conquer skittish Jack."

—Elisa Rolle

"I have only read one other book by Mr. Cade, but after reading *Treasure of Love* I am sure more of his books will show up on my TBR list."

—Top 2 Bottom Reviews

Foundation of Love

"An amazing story of love and courage, *Foundation of Love* by Scotty Cade and Z.B. Marshall will touch your heart and leave you breathless."

—Sensual Reads

By SCOTTY CADE

Published by DREAMSPINNER PRESS
http://www.dreamspinnerpress.com

An Unconventional Union

Scotty Cade

Dreamspinner Press

Published by
Dreamspinner Press
5032 Capital Circle SW
Ste 2, PMB# 279
Tallahassee, FL 32305-7886
USA
http://www.dreamspinnerpress.com/

An Unconventional Union

Cover Art by Reese Dante
http://www.reesedante.com

ISBN: 978-1-62380-385-8
Digital ISBN: 978-1-62380-386-5

Printed in the United States of America
First Edition
February 2013

As always, to my partner Kell. He's the one who always carries extra weight and makes sacrifices so I can put my stories to paper. I love you!

This book is also dedicated to our very dear friends, Norton Gerard and Stephen Locke. They are the inspiration for Tristan and Webber's love. They've been partners for over forty years and are still very much in love. Thank you for setting an example, not only for Tristan and Webber, but for Kell and me as well. We love you!

One

TRISTAN MOREAU lay in bed staring up at the pleated fabric pulled tightly from the center of the canopy and stretched to the ends of the large four-poster bed. Webber Kincaid, his lover of nearly a month and his boss for the last two years, was sleeping soundly beside him with his head resting on Tristan's chest and his arm draped over Tristan's stomach. With the rhythmic up and down motion of Webber's soothing breaths, Tristan was reminded of what he held in his arms. A little over an hour ago, they were making passionate love, and now, with the passion and desperate need temporarily sated, Tristan mimicked Webber's slow, even breathing as if they were one body sharing the same lungs. He looked at the diamond and emerald encrusted ring now gracing his right ring finger, amazed at how it caught the blue moonlight seeping in through the transom above the french doors. *Engaged!* Webber's words from earlier in the evening still echoed in Tristan's head: "Tristan Paul Moreau, I am at home only when I am in your arms and I'm more in love with you than I thought humanly possible. I want to be with you for the rest of my life. Make me the happiest man in the world and marry me."

Tristan smiled as he remembered how quickly his response had left his mouth. "Yes! Yes. Of course I'll marry you!" he'd said without even giving it a second thought.

He'd always had an issue with what he called the "brain to mouth" syndrome; whatever popped into his brain came out of his mouth. His response to Webber's proposal was no real exception. The "exception" was that most times he'd wished he could take back what he'd said the minute it left his mouth, but not this time. No way was he taking that back.

His smile turned into a full-out chuckle when he remembered how he'd almost knocked Webber to the floor when he'd thrown his arms around him, nearly squeezing the life out of him.

As Tristan lay there with the man he loved in his arms, his smile slowly faded and concern replaced the happiness. "Tris, I want to marry you as soon as possible," Webber had said right after Tristan had accepted his proposal.

He stroked Webber's hair as Webber slept soundly in his arms and wondered if the rush to marriage was because of the investigation by the SEC and the Department of Justice regarding Nathan Bridges, his former CFO. The thought of the SEC investigating Webber sent shivers up his spine. Did Webber really think there was a possibility that the SEC would think he had anything to do with Nathan's wrongdoings?

Tristan's mind started to drift back to when they'd met and how far they'd come in their relationship.

ENGAGED to Webber Kincaid was definitely not a turn of events he'd expected when he interviewed for the position as Webber's chief administrative assistant two years ago. Giving up his life in New York was difficult, but coming to work for Kincaid International Corporation, or KIC, was certainly worth it. Worth it in spite of Tristan's fears—quickly realized—that he could easily fall in love with his new, seemingly heterosexual, boss. Tristan couldn't tell Webber he loved him; he didn't want to risk his job or Webber's reputation, so he told himself he was content to care for Webber under the cloak of simply doing his job.

When Webber had returned early from a trip to Australia to review potential acquisitions with Nathan Bridges, KIC's then-CFO, he called Tristan to join him for a drink at the company lounge. Given that Tristan wasn't even expecting Webber to be back yet, he was a little surprised to hear from him. He was even more surprised when he heard what Webber was proposing—an extended trip to a private Caribbean island to review fifteen potential acquisitions without the interference of the Business Development or Finance departments. Tristan was unsure why Webber was asking him—and whether or not it would be a good idea—but in the end, the need to be close to Webber, even for work, won out, and Tristan agreed to accompany him, knowing they would have to work right through the weekend to complete all of their outstanding projects.

With a rush of excitement, Tristan smiled, remembering the powerful feeling of the helicopter vibrating under his feet and the feel of Webber's arm over his shoulder pointing out the different islands. And the view as they approached their destination: man, he'd never seen anything so beautiful. The island's lush green foliage was spectacular against the deep blue-green water. The sight reminded him of a pool of sapphires with handfuls of emeralds sprinkled here and there.

That weekend, as they worked together, Tristan kept wondering if he was imagining things, or if Webber really was subtly flirting with him. As far as he knew, Webber had a longtime girlfriend named Deanna Lynn. But his smile quickly lessened and eventually turned into a frown as he thought back to how elated he'd been by Webber's interest in him until he'd seen Deanna standing on the helicopter pad excitedly waving her hands in anticipation of their arrival. Shortly after they'd left Atlanta, Tristan had foolishly allowed himself to think, for just a second, that it would be he and Webber on this island alone together, but seeing Deanna had been a rude awakening and quickly crushed any stupid hopes he'd had of the man he loved ever being interested in him for anything more than an assistant.

But unbeknownst to Tristan, Webber *had* fallen in love with him, yet because of his position and the potential for a sexual harassment suit if Tristan wasn't gay or simply was not interested, Webber had never been able to tell him how he truly felt. After they got together, Webber confessed that although it truly was a working trip, Webber had hoped the time away would give him an opportunity to see if he could pick up on anything that might indicate where Tristan's sexual preferences lay. But just in case Tristan wasn't gay, Webber had invited

Deanna, his best friend and confidant, along on the trip as a decoy. That had badly backfired when Webber found the nerve to kiss Tristan, and Tristan, having been hurt by a similar relationship in the past, thought Webber was cheating on Deanna and couldn't be any part of that.

Tristan brushed the fingers of his free hand over his lips, remembering the feeling of Webber's lips pressed against his in the warm water of the swimming pool that evening so many months ago. But he also recalled the panic he'd felt when he realized what was happening. He gently stroked Webber's hair and kissed his temple, partly out of habit, but partly to reassure himself that Webber was still there and this wasn't a dream.

His mind wandered again, as he remembered he had been so upset by the thought that Webber could cheat on Deanna, he'd even gone so far as to resign. Of course, after some turmoil, Deanna had straightened everything out, and they were finally able to be honest with each other.

But now, Tristan wondered if he was going to lose Webber before they even really began. As the icing on the cake, their time away had become bittersweet, since Webber's now former CFO threatened to blackmail them because Webber had used the KIC corporate jet for a questionable business trip—although Webber had personally paid for all of the expenses associated with the trip.

TRISTAN was startled out of his thoughts by Webber's sleepy voice. "Tris, I can hear you thinking," he murmured. "Do you want to talk about it yet?"

"God, Web, sometimes I hate how well you know me. I'm sorry if I woke you."

"You didn't wake me." Webber leaned up on one elbow. "I was just dozing. Tell me what's bothering you?"

"I'm just worrying about the SEC. They can be relentless in their investigations."

"I figured as much. Please don't worry; it's not going to change the outcome."

"I was just remembering everything we've gone through to get here, and I can't lose you. Not now."

"You're not going to lose me, Tris," Webber reassured him. "I'm certain this is just a routine investigation, and I'll be cleared very soon."

Tristan sighed. "But tomorrow's the board of directors meeting. What if they decide you inappropriately used corporate resources for personal reasons? We both know it started out as a business trip, but it sure as hell didn't end that way. And on top of that, what if they decide you knew what Nathan was doing all along?"

"Well, to be honest, I don't really care what they decide," Webber said with conviction. "Not anymore."

Tristan raised a brow and turned his head to study Webber. "What do you mean?"

Webber dropped back down and again rested his head on Tristan's chest while he spoke. "Well, since I met you, KIC doesn't seem to be as important to me as it used to. I mean, for all of those years, KIC was all I had, my partner in many ways. But now that I have you, Tris, I want my life to be different."

"Different how?" Tristan asked. "I'm not sure I understand."

"For starters, I just keep thinking about my parents. They worked all their lives accumulating a fortune, and then they died way too soon without ever getting to enjoy the money. And now because of them, we have the opportunity to enjoy our lives without any financial worries. I don't want what happened to them to happen to us."

Tristan pulled Webber close against him and kissed the top of his head, inhaling the clean smell of sandalwood shampoo while he decided how to respond. Before he could say anything, he heard Webber's voice.

"Would you... consider retiring with me?" he asked speculatively.

"Retire," he murmured as he began to stroke Webber's hair again, mulling over his request. "I have to admit the idea does sound very enticing."

Webber reached for his hand and pulled it to his lips, kissing Tristan's palm. "We could do anything and go anywhere we wanted. We would have so much fun."

Tristan knew he would consider it. In fact, he would do anything for Webber if he thought that's what Webber really wanted. But he wondered how much of this was really Webber being unhappy at KIC and wanting to start a new life versus him preparing himself for the possibility of losing his job.

"Web, I have to ask you a question, and please promise me you'll be honest."

"Okay," Webber responded.

Tristan paused while he tried to put his feelings into words. "Did you propose to me because you think there's a possibility that you'll be indicted and could possibly go to jail?" he finally asked.

Webber rose up to one elbow again and used his other hand to turn Tristan's face so he could look him in the eyes. "No! Of course not," he said quickly. "I proposed to you because I love you. Tristan, please tell me you know that."

Tristan nodded his head, needing to hear the words.

"I know that," Tristan whispered.

"But," Webber continued, "I promised you that I would be honest with you and I will. I have no idea if the SEC or the Department of Justice will think I had anything to do with Nathan's indiscretions or what they'll do, but I want you to be taken care of in the event they don't believe I'm innocent and try to indict me."

Tristan sat up, his nervousness now getting the best of him. "So I was right. This urgency is all about the investigation."

Webber caressed Tristan's cheek with the back of his hand. "Tris, you know me better than that. How many times have you said that when I want something I go after it? Why would I be any different when it comes to you?"

Tristan's concern ebbed a little and he lay back down. "I just don't want to lose you, Web, and I don't want you to marry me just because you think you might be going away."

Tristan took note of the confidence when Webber next spoke. "You're not going to lose me. We both know I had nothing to do with my former CFO's activities, and the truth will come out."

Webber sighed then took Tristan's hand and pressed it to his cheek. "Baby, I love you and that's all that matters."

Tristan turned his head and kissed Webber's palm as his rapidly beating heart started returning to normal. "I love you too, Web. But I don't need taking care of."

Webber turned his head up and pressed his lips against Tristan's for a slow, gentle kiss. When the kiss ended, he pulled back and smiled at Tristan. "I always want to take care of you, but that doesn't mean I think you need taking care of. And just for the record, I knew I was going to ask you to marry me when we were still in the Caribbean. It has nothing to do with the SEC or the investigation, but everything to do with you and the way I feel about you."

Tristan couldn't help the smile that spread across his face. "In that case, let's do it as soon as possible. I can't wait to be Tristan Moreau-Kincaid."

Webber smiled. "I like the sound of that."

"Me too," Tristan said as he kissed Webber's temple.

THE next morning Webber stood in front of the full-length mirror tying his necktie. He looked exceptionally calm for a man about to be put under a microscope by a room full of his peers. Tristan walked up behind him, slid his hands around Webber's waist, and kissed the back of his neck. "You okay?" he asked.

Webber looked at Tristan in the mirror confidently. "Yeah, I am."

Tristan turned Webber around and slid the knot on his necktie up to Webber's collar and straightened it. "You look incredible. And you smell good too," he added, leaning in and taking a deep breath.

"Thanks. How about you, you nervous?"

"A little," Tristan admitted. "I do feel somewhat responsible since I'm the one you took to the Caribbean."

Webber smiled and took Tristan into his arms. "You are not responsible. I'm the one who invited you, remember?"

Tristan laughed nervously. "Okay, let's not split hairs."

Webber squeezed Tristan tighter and released him. "Tris, you realize I'm going to have to be completely honest with the board. That means outing both of us."

"I realize that, Web, and I'm fine with it," Tristan said rather adamantly. "I love you and I don't care who knows."

Webber leaned in and kissed him. "Thank you. I feel the same way. But if you think you'll be the least bit uncomfortable in that meeting, I can get someone else to sit in and take the minutes."

"Hell no," Tristan protested. "We do this together. And besides, taking the minutes of the board meetings is my job, and I'm gonna do it with my head held high until someone tells me I can't do it anymore or until I decide I no longer want to."

Webber chuckled. "I love you so much," he whispered as he pulled Tristan into his arms for another embrace.

Webber stepped back and looked Tristan in the eyes. "There are a few more things I wanted to talk to you about."

"Shoot," Tristan answered.

Webber didn't hesitate. "I don't know how this is going to go today, but I decided that whether or not I get to keep my job, *when* the SEC and the Department of Justice clear me, I'm gonna resign." Webber paused. "If it's okay with you, that is."

Tristan raised an eyebrow, taking note of the "when" and happy Webber hadn't said "if." "Are you sure that's what you want?"

"I am," Webber offered. "I've thought about it a lot. KIC is no longer the company my dad and I ran. In the back of my mind, I knew that would happen when I took it public, but it was the best thing for the company and my father's legacy, so I did it."

"Then I'll support you one hundred percent," Tristan said.

Webber took Tristan's hands in his. "Which brings me to my next question."

"The answer's yes, Web."

"What do you mean, 'yes'?" Webber asked. "I haven't said anything yet."

"You don't have to," Tristan assured him. "I'll resign with you."

Webber grabbed Tristan around the waist, picked him up, spun him around, and put him back down on his feet. "We are going to have such a great life, Tris."

"I know it," Tristan said. "So is that all the significant stuff?"

"Almost," Webber confirmed with a more serious look on his face. "The last thing is the press conference."

Tristan tilted his head to one side. "What about it?" he asked.

"Well, once we go public with our news, it's going to get crazy for a while. The paparazzi are going to go wild over this, and I want to make sure you're prepared."

Tristan mulled over his answer. "I suppose I'm as prepared as I can be."

"Look, Tris, we don't have to do this. If this bothers you, we have another option."

"What's that?" Tristan asked.

"We can lay low, *not* out ourselves, and wait until someone outs us."

"It's not the outing that bothers me," Tristan confessed. "It's the fact that our lives might not be our own for a while."

"Whatever you want to do is fine by me," Webber said. "But we either pay the piper now or pay him later."

"I say we go for it and get on with our lives," Tristan proposed. "I don't want us looking over our shoulder every time we leave the house."

"I see your point," Webber agreed. "I say we go for it too."

"Then it's settled," Tristan said as he raised his arms and locked them behind Webber's neck. "We're in this together, for better or for worse, 'til death do us part."

Webber chuckled. "Those words sound very familiar."

"They better," Tristan teased. "We're gonna be saying them very soon."

THEY decided to take Webber's car into work, neither of them caring if anyone saw them arriving together. When they reached the closed boardroom door, Webber stopped and turned to Tristan. "You ready, Tris?"

"As ready as I'll ever be," Tristan said in shaky voice.

"Let's do this," Webber said as he nervously pushed the door open. Two of the six board members were already seated and stood up when they saw Webber and Tristan enter.

"Scott," Webber said, extending his hand. "Nice to see you."

"Good morning," Tristan said to Scott, extending his hand as well.

Scott Mullin was the chief financial officer of Restaurant Group South, a large chain of high-end restaurants, and had been on the board for four years.

"Gentlemen," Scott said, sheepishly looking at Webber and Tristan. "Nice to see you both, but I wish it were under better circumstances."

Webber nodded and smiled. "Tell me about it."

Webber watched as Tristan gracefully moved on to the next board member.

"Ms. Jordan, how are you?" Tristan said, shaking the woman's hand.

"Fine, Tristan, thanks for asking."

Hillary Jordan was the president and CEO of Landscape America and was a personal friend of Webber's late mother and father. She'd been the first person Webber called to sit on his board when he decided to take the company public.

"Hillary," Webber said, putting his hand on her shoulder. "Good to see you. How's Paul?"

"He's good, Webber," Hillary said. "We're a bit surprised by all of this, but we'll get through it. You know we're on your side." She looked at Tristan and smiled.

"Thanks, Hil," Webber said, looking between her and Tristan. "You have no idea how much that means to us."

Before Webber could say anything else, three more board members appeared in the doorway: John Reynolds, president of HomeCare, a nationwide home improvement store, Cynthia Bowen, chief marketing officer for Talk US, a cellular provider, and Betty Katz, chief operating officer for the local ABC affiliate. Before everyone could say their hellos, the final board member, Robert Yellos, chairman of the board for Global Media Corp, a broadcast media buying company appeared, not looking too happy. After greetings were exchanged, Webber moved to his seat and Tristan to his position in the corner of the room at a small desk designed for him to quietly take the minutes of the board meeting.

Webber called the meeting to order. "Ladies and gentlemen," he said. "I thank each of you for taking the time out of your busy schedules to attend this unscheduled meeting of the board for KIC. As you are all aware, Nathan Bridges has confessed to inflating the cost of one particular acquisition we made back in 2005 and divested in 2007, and was trying to guide us to purchase the company again, which has now changed its name and moved Down Under. We are also here to discuss a discretionary business trip taken by Tristan and myself, which may or may not have been appropriate. But we will get to that later. Before we discuss what action may be taken toward me or KIC by the SEC and the Department of Justice, I'd like to play the recording of Nathan's confession. I don't have to remind you that in the state of Georgia, a recording can be admissible in a court of law if at least one person knows the conversation is being recorded. Here we go," Webber said as he pressed the "on" button on his recorder.

"WHAT can I do for you, Nathan?"

"I've been told that you requested the file for the divestiture of Marquis Advertising."

"That's right."

"May I ask why?"

"I'm doing a little research," they heard Webber respond.

"Come on, Webber, we've known each other too long to play games."

"I'm not playing games; I'm just trying to do my job."

"Really?" Nathan said sarcastically. "First, you held back the Moniker Communications file when you turned over all of the other potential acquisitions to Finance, then you checked out the acquisition file for Marquis Advertising, and then you requested the file for the divestiture of Marquis. I'm not stupid, Webber. That's a very strange coincidence.

"We're adults here, Webber, let's put all our cards on the table and be honest."

They didn't hear Webber respond.

"Okay. I'll go first," Nathan said. "How did you find out?"

"Find out what?"

There was a loud sound like someone slamming a hand on a desk.

"You know exactly what I'm talking about and I want to know what you're going to do about it."

"How did you do it?" Webber asked.

"Oh, it was simple actually. I merely convinced the owner of Marquis to inflate the asking price then supply me with a list of bogus contracts to support that price and we'd split the difference. Clean and simple."

They heard Webber speak next. "But why risk everything? You make a good living here."

"I needed money," Nathan responded. "I was in the middle of a divorce, being taken for everything, and my girlfriend wanted more and more."

Webber's voice was clear. "And you might have gotten away with it if you hadn't gone back for a second round. Did you really think I wouldn't put two and two together?"

"Hey, can't blame a guy for trying," Nathan said. "I'm curious, though, how did you find me out?"

"Actually Tristan did, but only because he looked at the Moniker files before I had a chance to. It turns out that when I was mentoring him on evaluating acquisitions, I gave him a handful of KIC's previous acquisitions to review and Marquis happened to be one of them. So when he was reviewing the files for Moniker, he recognized the client list and financials."

"I'm impressed," Nathan admitted "I didn't give the twit enough credit."

Webber laughed. "You're calling him a twit? But I must admit you seem awfully calm for a man about to be in very big trouble."

"Oh, I don't think I'm in that much trouble," Nathan said with confidence in his voice.

"Really, why not?" was Webber's response.

"Well, because if I go down, you go down right along with me," Nathan warned. "You signed off on the transaction, remember."

"I remember the argument we had over this transaction and you producing a series of contracts supporting the purchase price," Webber said. "But I had no idea those contracts were fabricated and worth nothing."

"It's your word against mine now, isn't it? Come on, Webber," Nathan said. "That transaction was a long time ago. If you keep your mouth shut, no one will ever be the wiser."

"I'm afraid I can't do that," Webber responded.

"I'm sorry to hear that, because that leaves me no choice but to out you and that twit back there," Nathan said.

"What are you talking about, Nathan?"

"There you go playing games with me again, Webber," he hissed. "I think the board will be happy to learn that you've been cavorting around the Caribbean on company resources with an employee of yours, doing who knows what," he threatened. "I've always suspected you two had something going on. I could just tell by the way you looked at each other, but I didn't know for sure until your little display of affection in the parking lot yesterday. Thanks for giving me some leverage."

"What Tristan and I do behind closed doors is no concern of yours or the board's."

"You're quite right, but what you're forgetting is when you use corporate resources to fund your little rendezvous, that becomes a very different story."

"Nathan, you know perfectly well we were on a legitimate business trip," Webber insisted. "We evaluated fifteen potential acquisitions in a quarter of the time it would have taken your business development department to do it."

"Oh, Webber, you disappoint me sometimes. The reasons why have nothing to do with it," Nathan said. "You took a personal trip on a company-owned jet with an employee with whom you were romantically involved. That doesn't bode well in your favor at all."

"Webber, you just think about it for a little while and we'll talk again before the end of the day. I'm sure when you think this through, you'll agree it's better for everyone if we both keep our mouths shut and forget this ever happened."

They heard silence and then a door slam.

"SO THIS is what the SEC and the Department of Justice have," Webber stated. "My attorney says it is admissible in court and will, in the end, clear me of any wrongdoing. Any comments?"

The board members looked at each other and Hillary was the first to speak. "It appears to me from what we just heard regarding this matter that, pending any other evidence, you are in the clear."

"I agree," Scott added.

John, Cynthia, and Betty all nodded in Webber's favor.

Robert cleared his voice. "How could you not know that those contracts were bogus?"

Before Webber could answer, Scott spoke up. "How would he know? He questioned his CFO like he should have and his CFO fed him bad information. Short of calling each of those contracts to make sure they were legit, there is no way he could have known. Would you have verified every contract?"

"Come on," Betty added. "We all trust our CFO. If we didn't, they wouldn't be in the position. Webber has a great track record here and I believe he will be vindicated."

Webber stood. "I appreciate everyone's kind words, but I did sign that contract and I am ultimately responsible, so I'm not trying to dodge a bullet here. The issue at hand, though, is if I was negligent or not, and I do not believe I was. I did my homework and I asked the right questions. Hell, I even fought with Nathan about the price. When he produced executed contracts, I had no choice but to propose it to you for approval."

"I say we put it to a vote," Cynthia suggested. "Is everyone in agreement that we show a united front to the SEC and the Department of Justice and support our chairman, president, and CEO?"

Webber looked over at Tristan, his heart racing. He watched Tristan close his eyes and sigh when they both heard "ayes" from all the board members, although a reluctant one from Robert Yellos.

He smiled and winked at Tristan before turning back to the board. "Thank you," he said. "I appreciate your support. Does anyone want to take a break before we move on to the next issue at hand?"

Everyone looked around, but no one moved. "Okay then," Webber said. "Moving on to the next order of business."

Webber glanced over at Tristan and took a deep breath before he spoke. "The next matter is of a very personal nature and may be difficult for some of you to hear or understand, but it's important to us that you know the truth. Although my personal life and whom I spend it with is of no one's concern but mine, I want to tell you the complete story and then allow you to decide if I acted inappropriately or not. If you find that I did act inappropriately, I will accept whatever consequences you deem appropriate and not take it personally."

Webber again looked over at Tristan, who seemed to have lost most of his color but was holding it together very nicely. "My, I mean, our," Webber corrected, "story began a couple of years ago when Tristan Moreau, who you all know very well, joined KIC as my chief administrative assistant. On my part, there was an immediate attraction and for reasons I didn't understand at the time, I still made him an offer and ultimately hired him. Unbeknownst to me, Tristan had the same initial attraction and over the last two years, we managed to fall head over heels in love with each other."

The board members again looked around the room at each other, but no one made any comment.

"However, during those two years, neither of us acted upon our attractions for fear of what the outcome might be. From Tristan's standpoint, he wasn't sure that I was gay, so he was fearful of losing his job, and if I was gay, he was concerned for my reputation and the reputation of KIC if he acted on his feelings. From my standpoint, I didn't know what his personal preferences were, and not wanting to open myself or KIC up for a sexual harassment suit, I kept my feelings to myself. The longer we worked together, the harder it became for me to hide my feelings, so I decided to try and get a handle on where Tristan's head was."

Webber paused and poured himself a glass of water, taking a sip and then putting the glass down in front of him. He glanced around the room and smiled, appearing to have everyone's attention and even a little sympathy from a few of the board members, mostly the women.

"As most of you know, I'd just returned from a trip Down Under to look at possible acquisitions, and although we discovered fifteen possibilities, you as a board had only approved five for the remainder of the fiscal year. I wanted to sort through the fifteen before I gave them to the business development department and decided to take a much-needed working vacation. I've shared with some of you that I was mentoring Tristan in acquisitions and divestures and he had a knack for it, so I invited him along to help me sort through the mounds of paperwork. And I know what you're thinking: it was a way to spend time alone with Tristan and you are right. I'd be lying if I said it wasn't. But all I wanted was a little time to see if I could figure out where Tristan's sexual preferences lay to determine if I would at some point approach him with my feelings. Fortunately for us, I got my answer and we've been inseparable ever since. As a matter of fact, I proposed, he accepted, and we will be married very shortly. But, please allow me to be very clear. I did nothing inappropriate, what we did was between consenting adults, and in the end, we sorted through all fifteen potential acquisitions with Tristan discovering that something wasn't right with Marquis/Moniker. Furthermore, I did use the company jet, but I paid for all expenses surrounding the trip with no costs to KIC. In the folder in front of you, you will find my credit card statements with all expenses highlighted in yellow pertaining to this trip."

Webber stopped then took a deep breath and another sip of his water. "Any questions?"

Hillary was the first to speak. "I know you said that neither of you acted on your attraction during the two years leading up to the trip to the Caribbean, but it's very important that you tell us the truth. If we chose to support you and something to the contrary is leaked—" She paused and looked around the room at the other board members. "— none of us will be very pleased. Come on, Webber, if your relationship is anything like my relationship with my personal assistant, I'm sure you must have worked many long nights together and had many opportunities."

"Yes, we have had many opportunities, but the answer is still no," Webber assured her and the other board members. "Unless you consider sharing a scotch after a very long day acting on feelings."

Before Hillary could respond, Scott spoke next. "So, you are right in that your personal life does not affect your ability to do your job, but you must know that it would be very questionable for us to allow Tristan to be your personal assistant knowing what we now know."

Webber nodded.

Scott continued. "But the real issue I see here for us to determine is if you used company resources for personal interest."

"He's already said he invited Tristan to join him to try and gauge his sexual preference," Robert said. "That to me screams personal interest."

"Yes," Cynthia said. "But he also worked while he was away and in the end, caught Nathan in some very heavy deceptions."

John Reynolds had been quiet up until now. "Look, ladies and gentlemen, Webber has done nothing but run this company and run it well for a very long time. Yes, this was a questionable decision, but are we prepared to terminate a damn good man because of one questionable decision?"

No one answered.

"Thank you, John," Webber said. "But maybe it's time for Tristan and me to step out and allow you to speak more freely. Hillary, will you please take notes so we can incorporate them into our minutes when this is all over?"

She nodded and smiled.

Webber held out his hand to Tristan, and he accepted it as they walked out of the boardroom and closed the door behind him.

"Well," Tristan asked. "What do you think?"

"Your guess is as good as mine," Webber said. "Hillary and John seem sympathetic, Robert as always is a pain in the ass, and I couldn't get a read on Scott, Cynthia, or Betty."

"Am I going to lose my job?" Tristan asked.

"I'm sorry, Tris. It appears that way, but by no fault of your own. I take full responsibility," Webber admitted. "But since we're going to retire, I don't think it matters one way or the other."

Tristan appeared to think this over. "I guess you're right," he said, shrugging.

"That's my boy," Webber said, pulling him into a hug.

Just then the door opened and Hillary invited them back in.

Webber didn't release Tristan, but instead led him to the head of the table where they stood hand in hand and awaited their fate.

"Please take a seat, gentlemen," Scott offered.

"Thank you," Webber said. "But if it's all the same, I think we'll stand."

Scott nodded and began. "After listening to your heartfelt and very honest confession, we as the board, not unanimously I might add, believe your account and believe you did not set out to deceive KIC's board, its employees, or its shareholders in any way, shape, or form."

Webber closed his eyes, sighed, and squeezed Tristan's hand.

Scott continued looking at Tristan. "It is, however, unfortunate that Mr. Moreau will not be allowed to keep his job as your personal assistant and must be laterally moved into another department where he will have no interaction with you in a professional capacity."

Tristan nodded and squeezed Webber's hand.

Webber looked around the boardroom. Everyone was smiling, but Hillary and John were beaming. "Congratulations, gentlemen," John said. "We wish you the best."

Webber nodded as he glanced at Tristan, barely able to contain himself. "Thank you all very much, and I appreciate the faith you've put in me over the years and the support you've shown us today. I've enjoyed working with each of you and want only the best for KIC. To that end, Tristan and I would like to turn in our resignations, Tristan's immediate and mine as soon as the SEC and/or the Department of Justice clears me and you can find a suitable replacement. You'll each have a copy of my resignation letter by tomorrow morning."

Webber saw the shocked looks on the faces of every board member.

"What?" Hillary asked. "But...."

Webber put his hands up. "May I speak freely?"

"Please," John responded.

"I've not been happy for a while, and I've been considering this move for quite some time. But in light of the recent developments and accusations, I want to be cleared of any wrongdoing before I resign. I've had a great track record, and I don't want that tarnished by a scandal."

Webber looked around the room for any indication of how they were taking the news. "In addition, because of my philanthropy and my position here, I'm heavily covered in the media, so as soon as I'm cleared, Tristan and I will be giving a press conference to confirm our relationship before TMZ or some other tabloid reporter outs us and we have to do damage control."

Still no one said a word. "In addition I would like to have a staff meeting for my direct reports and explain the situation before they hear it in the news. They deserve that. I'd love your input and your support for both, but we will move forward with or without it."

"Of course," Hillary said, looking around and getting nods from the other board members. "But we have to handle this very carefully."

Webber put one arm over Tristan's shoulder and looked at the board members again. "You can decide how much or how little involvement you want from me until you find a suitable replacement. My exit package is on record, so I don't expect to have any issues there. If you need me in the meantime, I will be reachable by cell phone."

Webber removed his arm from Tristan's shoulder and brought his hands together with his fingertips touching. "Ladies and gentlemen of the board," he said. "Unless you have any other questions…?" Webber looked around the boardroom, waiting for any sort of response. When the room remained silent, Webber said, "This meeting is adjourned."

He threw his arms around Tristan's neck and whispered, "I love you. Let's get the hell out of here."

They bolted for the door and once they were in the hall, Webber lifted Tristan from the waist and spun him around like a twelve-year-old. "We did it," he said, almost giddy.

"Web, put me down," Tristan begged. "They'll be plenty of time for celebration later; we're still at the office."

Webber did as he was told, and Tristan regained his footing about the same time the boardroom door opened and Hillary stepped out. "I guess congratulations are in order," she said, hugging Webber. She turned to Tristan and smiled. "I'm very happy for you both and I wish you the best of luck," she added. "Tristan, do you mind if I have a word with Webber?"

"Not at all," Tristan said. "I need to pack my office anyway. Meet me there, Web?"

Webber smiled and kissed Tristan on the cheek. "Will do, baby," he said.

As soon as Tristan was out of earshot, Hillary smacked him on the shoulder. "Webber Kincaid, how could you not tell me something like this?"

Webber smiled and rubbed his shoulder. "Because it was a nonissue," Webber responded. "Until now, that is."

Hillary chuckled. "Still, you could have told me," she whined. "But I must say, you do look happier than I've seen you in years."

Webber corrected her. "No, I'm happier than I've ever been."

She took both his hands in hers. "And I'm happy for you. Promise me you boys will come over and have dinner with Paul and me. We need to get to know Tristan better."

"We'll do that, Hil," Webber promised. "But first we're gonna take some time, find a place to get married, and do a little traveling."

"That sounds nice," Hillary said. "I hope we'll be on the invitation list for the wedding."

"Of course you will." Webber paused. "I just wish...." His voice trailed off.

Hillary finished his sentence. "You wish your parents could be there."

Webber nodded and a single tear slid down his cheek.

Hillary wiped the tear away and kissed him tenderly. "They'll be there in spirit, don't you worry."

"Thanks, Hil."

Hillary hugged him. "I need to get back in there and see what we're going to do about replacing you."

Just as Hillary put her hand on the doorknob, the door opened.

"Oh, sorry, Hillary," John Reynolds said as he stepped out of the boardroom. "I just wanted to congratulate Webber before he left."

Hillary smiled. "Okay, I'll give you two a little privacy," she said as she went back in to join the other board members.

"Thanks, John," Webber said. "I really appreciate your support back in there."

"Hey look, no problem," John said. "You've done a great job here, and I'm truly sorry to see you go."

John bounced from one foot to the other and Webber thought he looked a little nervous. "Thank you, John," he said as he offered his hand for a shake.

John accepted it and they shook, John hanging on a little longer than usual. "Is there something else, John?" Webber asked.

"Well, I, ah, just wanted to invite you and Tristan to dine with Charles and me at the Buckhead Club sometime," he stammered.

"Charles?" Webber asked, a little confused.

"My husband."

Webber raised an eyebrow. "John, are you telling me that you're gay?"

John looked around the hall to make sure they were still alone. "Yep," he replied. "Charles and I have been together for twelve years, married for two."

"How did I not know this?" Webber asked.

"I guess for the same reason I didn't know about you," John responded.

"Touché." Webber laughed. "I'm sure we'd like that," Webber said. "As I told Hillary, we're going to take a little time off, look for a place to get married, and travel for a while, but we would love to spend some time with you guys when we return."

"Sounds good," John said. "But hey, before I get back in there, I'd like to suggest a little place for your wedding. Have you ever been to Martha's Vineyard?"

"I've heard of the island, but I've never been there," Webber admitted.

"Great place, secluded and private. There's a little place called the Inn at Lambert's Cove and it's really beautiful. You know gay marriage has been legal in Massachusetts since 2004, and Charles and I were married there. It's owned by a gay couple, and they did a great job for us."

"Sounds wonderful," Webber said genuinely. "I'll tell Tristan and we'll look it up later tonight. Thanks for the tip."

"My pleasure," John said with a pat on the back. "I'd better get back in there and help them figure all this out. Good luck, Webber."

"Okay, and thanks again," Webber said, still stunned at John's admission.

TRISTAN had just finished going through his files, placing his personal items in a file box, and was about to start packing away his small stereo when it really sunk in that he would no longer be coming to this office every day. He sat in the chair opposite his desk and looked around. No more late nights and weekends taking off his shoes, turning up his stereo, and getting lost in his work. He'd spent some of the best times of his career and his life in this office working with Webber, loving Webber from afar, and he realized how much he was going to miss it. But a smile formed on his face; knowing he was going to spend the rest of his life with Webber instead of simply working for him was so much better.

He was startled out of his thoughts by a hand lightly resting on his shoulder. He turned to see Webber standing behind him smiling weakly. "You okay?" Webber asked.

Tristan nodded. "Yeah, just doing a little reminiscing."

"You want some time alone?"

"No, it's okay," Tristan responded. "I've just spent so many long enjoyable hours here with you that I'm really going to miss this place."

"I'm so sorry. Tris, all this is my fault," Webber said as he gently massaged Tristan's shoulders.

Tristan laid a hand on top of one of Webber's. "It's no one's fault, Web," Tristan assured him. "And just for the record, if I had to choose between spending the rest of my life with you or keeping my job, you win hands down."

Webber kissed the top of Tristan's head. "Thanks, baby, I feel the same way. Now what can I do to help?"

"You can start packing up those CDs while I pack up the stereo," Tristan instructed. "How did it go after I left?"

"Hillary was great. She wants us to spend some time with her and Paul. But that's not the shocker."

Tristan held a stereo speaker in his hand, about to start wrapping it up when he stopped and looked at Webber.

Webber simply smiled.

"What?" Tristan asked in an impatient tone.

"If I told you one of our board members is gay, who would you choose?" Webber asked, still smiling.

Tristan thought about the question. He knew the board members pretty well, and he ran down a mental list of their marital statuses. "John Reynolds?" he guessed.

"Bingo," Webber said, his smile broadening.

"Get out," Tristan responded.

"How did you guess?" Webber asked.

"I started with him because he's the only one that's single," Tristan said as he started wrapping the speaker again.

"You're so smart," Webber teased. "But he's not single. He has a husband named Charles, and they've been together twelve years. Oh, and they were married a couple of years ago at a place on Martha's Vineyard, and John said it's very private and secluded."

Tristan placed the wrapped speaker in the box and reached for the second one. "Isn't that the island off the coast of Massachusetts where President Obama and his family vacation?"

"That's the place," Webber answered.

"Maybe we can look it up on the Internet tonight," Tristan suggested.

"Perfect," Webber said. "But as your last official task, can you call my direct reports and set up a meeting in twenty minutes while I go pack up a few things in my office?"

"Yes, sir," Tristan said with a mock salute.

Thirty minutes later, Webber and his direct reports, minus Nathan, were seated in Webber's office around the small conference table. Webber explained to them everything that had happened over the last couple of days and what they could expect in the near future regarding the investigation. He answered all their questions as best he could and asked them to be honest, straightforward, and cooperative with the SEC and the Department of Justice if they were questioned. Then he told them about his and Tristan's relationship and their resignation. Everyone was shocked about Nathan's activities, but seemed very supportive of Webber and Tristan, although sorry to see them both go. He also asked everyone to be as supportive of his replacement as they had been of him and assured each of them that their jobs were secure and KIC's future was very strong. The meeting ended with everyone a little dazed and confused, but they all wished Webber well on the way out of his office.

Webber was silent as he threw a few things in a box then sat down behind his desk and rubbed his temples. He looked up to see Tristan standing in front of his desk and their eyes locked in silence. When Webber finally spoke, his voice was a little strained. "Well, I think that went as well as could be expected," he concluded.

Tristan moved behind Webber at his desk and put his hand on his shoulder. "I'm glad. You know they respect you, Web. They always have."

Webber covered Tristan's hand with his own. "Thanks. What do you say we get the hell out of here, find a place for lunch, and start planning a wedding? I can get this stuff later."

Still at Webber's side, Tristan dropped to one knee then brought Webber's palm to his lips and gently kissed it. "Sounds like the perfect plan," he assured him. "I just need to stop by my office and get a couple of boxes."

Two

WEBBER and Tristan had just pulled out of the KIC parking garage when Webber's phone rang. He quickly glanced at the caller ID, and it was a Washington number. "I'll bet it's the SEC," he said.

He pulled the car into the visitor parking lot, turned off the radio, cleared his throat, and answered the call. "Webber Kincaid."

"Mr. Kincaid, this is Commissioner Dan Gallagher with the US Securities and Exchange Commission. Is this a good time?"

"I'm in the car just leaving the office, but sure," Webber replied.

"Is it possible for you to be in DC tomorrow for an informal hearing concerning Kincaid International?" the commissioner asked.

"I can do that," Webber indicated. "But can I ask if this has anything to do with an indictment against me?"

"That has not been determined as of yet," the commissioner offered. "But I would like you to be here in person to answer a few more questions and to go over what we've found out so far regarding our investigation."

Webber sighed. "What time tomorrow?"

"Eleven o'clock," the commissioner said.

"I'll be there. I assume it will be appropriate to have my attorney present."

"That won't be necessary as we already have your formal statement, but if you'll feel more comfortable, you can bring him along or conference him in by phone."

"Fine," Webber said. "I'll do that."

"Thank you, Mr. Kincaid. Until tomorrow then," the commissioner offered cheerfully.

Webber tapped the "End" on his cellphone and looked over at Tristan. "Looks like we're going to Washington DC tomorrow," he said as he pulled out of visitor parking.

Tristan rested his hand on Webber's thigh. "Did they say what they want to see you about?"

"Nope, just that they have a few more questions and want to go over what they've found so far," Webber explained. "Do you have Georgia Jet's number in your phone?"

Tristan was already searching his phone as Webber spoke. "One step ahead of you, Web," Tristan said as he selected the contact and initiated the call. "What time do you want to leave?" Tristan asked while the call connected.

"Let's see," Webber said, thinking out loud. "The flight time is a little over an hour if I remember correctly. Add in travel time from the airport to downtown DC, probably about eight thirty, I guess."

Webber could hear Tristan's soft voice making the arrangements in the background, but his mind had already wandered back to the SEC. *Why do they want to see me in person? If they were planning to clear me, they could have done that on the phone. This doesn't look good.*

When Webber tuned back into Tristan's voice, he heard him finishing the call. "Thank you very much, we'll be ready at eight thirty."

Tristan turned to Webber. "We're all set. The car will pick us up at eight o'clock and we're scheduled to take off shortly after that."

"Thanks for making the arrangements," Webber said as he put his hand on Tristan's shoulder and squeezed without ever taking his eyes off the road. "And thanks for coming with me."

Tristan smiled at him. "We're in this together, remember?"

"I know," Webber agreed. "But I'm still getting used to having someone to count on."

"Well, get used to it, because I'm not going anywhere," Tristan promised.

You going anywhere is not what I'm worried about. Webber kept that thought to himself. No sense in scaring Tristan any more than he already had until they knew what they were dealing with. Instead he said, "What do you say we hit Buckhead Diner for a nice, leisurely lunch?"

Tristan took Webber's free hand in his and held it in his lap. "I'd like that," he said.

THEY were a little after the lunch crowd, so they got a table right away. For starters, they ordered Bloody Marys and house-made blue cheese potato chips, one of the Buckhead Diner's specialties, to snack on, and for entrées they both ordered grilled chicken cobb salads. Webber brought his iPad with him, and while they waited for their lunch, they searched for the wedding venue on Martha's Vineyard that John Reynolds had told Webber about.

"Here it is," Webber said. "The Inn at Lambert's Cove."

Tristan scooted his chair over as Webber pulled up the website. "Wow," he said when he saw the homepage. "This place looks gorgeous."

Webber quietly read the overview from the homepage.

"There is no lovelier setting, indoors or out, than the Inn at Lambert's Cove for a wedding reception, anniversary celebration, or other special event. The estate dates back to 1790, and as you enter the front door and foyer, you are immediately aware of the English country décor accented by warm colors and elegant but comfortable furnishings. To your left you'll see our comfortably stylish Red Room, decorated with mahogany leather furnishings with several cozy sitting areas for reading, listening to music, or just relaxing in front of the fireplace. To your right you'll note the more formal Club Room decorated in dark green, royal blue, and just a hint of gold. Straight ahead and to the right lie the library and main dining rooms with fireplaces, a hundred-year-old grand piano, and french doors opening out onto the beautiful salt mineral pool, spa, and expansive patio. The main house has seven beautifully decorated guest rooms, with our newly renovated carriage house and guesthouse holding eight additional guest rooms. The Inn can accommodate small intimate weddings and special events for two or more, and larger events with up to three hundred guests. Outside, the estate's picturesque grounds and gardens, all surrounded by 150-year-old vine-covered stone walls, await your leisurely stroll."

Tristan listened carefully until Webber was through reading. "This place sounds amazing. It's beautiful, secluded, and sounds just like what we're looking for."

"I agree," Webber said. "Why don't we call and make an appointment to tour the place tomorrow after we finish in DC?"

Tristan's eyes lit up. "Really, can we?" he asked.

"Sure," Webber answered. "It's a short flight. We can hop over, tour the place, spend the night, and then fly home the next morning."

"Sounds like a plan," Tristan said, munching on a potato chip.

On the way home from lunch, Tristan called Georgia Jet and rearranged their return, making a stop on Martha's Vineyard, then he called the Inn and spoke to one of the owners. He made a reservation for an overnight stay and a wedding tour, explaining that they weren't quite sure what time they would arrive, but that they would be in touch the next day as soon as their schedule was more definite.

When they got home, Webber pulled into the drive, punched the code into the security gate, and drove through. He watched inquisitively in his rearview mirror as a familiar car drove in behind them before the gate could close. "It appears we have company," Webber said, still looking in his rearview mirror. "And I think it's Nathan."

Tristan turned in his seat to get a better look and confirmed Webber's suspicions.

Instead of parking out front, not knowing what to expect from his former CFO, Webber drove around the back of the house and pulled the car into the garage then closed the door behind them. By the time they entered the house, he could hear a loud knocking on the front door. "I'll get it, Sophie," Webber called to his longtime housekeeper, hoping to get to the door before she did. "Stay here, Tristan. I have no idea what frame of mind he's in."

"But—"

Webber held up his hand. "This is not up for discussion," he said over his shoulder as he made his way to the foyer.

"Like hell it's not," Tristan said, following Webber down the hall to the foyer.

Webber stopped and turned around, blocking Tristan from going any farther. "Tris, I have no idea where his head is and don't want to provoke him by flaunting you, us, in his face. Remember you're the one who discovered his indiscretions. Please?"

"This conversation is not over," Tristan said as he turned and went into the kitchen.

As Webber approached the foyer, he knew he was too late. He could hear Nathan talking to Sophie.

"I'll take it from here, Sophie," Webber explained. "That will be all."

Sophie smiled and retreated down the hall. When she was out of sight, Webber spoke quietly. "What are you doing here, Nathan?" he asked incredulously, catching the strong scent of alcohol on Nathan's breath.

It appeared Nathan was wound up so tightly he might blow any second. He bounced from one foot to the other, fidgeting with his hands and not able to keep still. "I'm out on bail. I assume you're not taping me this time," he said nervously, looking around the foyer.

Webber didn't answer. "I don't think it's a good idea that you're here. You should probably go, Nathan," he said as he opened the front door and stood to the side, gesturing for Nathan to leave. But Nathan didn't budge. He folded his arms across his chest and planted both feet firmly on the floor, Webber assumed, in an attempt to look intimidating.

"I'm not leaving until I say what I came here to say."

No longer attempting to be nice, Webber closed the door and leaned back against it. "Fine, have your say, then get out or I'm calling the police, the SEC, and the Department of Justice."

Nathan's stance went from intimidating to seemingly small and frail. "Can't we come to some sort of arrangement, Webber?" he asked. "We've known each other for a long time, and I worked for your father. Please don't let me go to jail."

"You're right," Webber agreed. "And I think my father would be just as appalled as I am by your fraudulent activities and disloyalty. And then to try and blackmail Tristan and me."

Nathan threw his hands up in the air. "I—I'm sorry about that, Webber. I truly am. I would never have followed through with any of that. But I was in a bad place and made a stupid mistake."

Webber did his best to keep his calm. "You know what, Nathan," he said. "I can almost believe that."

Nathan sighed. "Thank you," he murmured. "Does that mean you'll help me?"

Webber raised both hands, palms out. "You didn't allow me to finish," he said, staring at Nathan with disdain. "As I said, I can almost believe you when you say you made a mistake and regret what you did. I mean… I get that we all make mistakes when we're under a lot of pressure. I do. But for you to do it all over again, that makes me crazy. You must think I'm so terribly stupid that you could do it all again with the same company and I wouldn't catch it. You must have had a lot of laughs at my expense over the first one, but I'm the one who's laughing last."

"It's not like that. Webber, I swear it's not," Nathan tried to explain.

Webber opened the door again. "Give it a rest, Nathan. We're done here. Now please leave."

"Please, Webber," Nathan begged. "Don't let me go to jail."

"I have no control over what happens to you," Webber explained. "My only crime here is that I trusted you. My bad!"

The look on Nathan's face quickly went from one of pleading to one of anger and resentment. "I'll get you for this, Webber. I'll tell the SEC that you knew about this all along and shared in the money."

Webber smiled. "You do that," he said. "They have a recording of you saying otherwise."

Nathan eyes were now cold and cunning. "That recording has me saying that it's your word against mine, and in fact, don't count on that recording to clear you because my lawyer is certain it will not be admissible evidence."

Webber smiled again. "Then your lawyer is as much of an idiot as you are," he warned. "The Georgia law is quite clear on the matter of taping a conversation. As long as at least one of the parties being taped knows the conversation is being recorded, it is totally legal and very admissible. And since I'm the one who was recording the conversation, we're all set."

Nathan's eyes narrowed. "I'll get you for this, Webber Kincaid," he said as he stormed across the foyer and out the front door. "This is not over," he yelled over his shoulder as Webber slammed the door.

Before Webber could turn around, he felt a strong hand on his shoulder. He turned and Tristan was standing behind him, and Sophie was near the hallway holding a large sauté pan.

"We heard everything, Web," Tristan confirmed. "I made Sophie listen as well in case we needed a witness."

"And I was ready," Sophie said, waving the sauté pan in the air.

Webber stepped back and looked at them, smiling. "Good thinking, you two, and Sophie, remind me to stay on your good side."

Sophie nodded and smiled, tapping the pan against the palm of her hand. "You remember that, Mr. Kincaid."

Webber's smile faded. "Did you hear the desperation in his voice and see the look in his eyes? They were empty and hollow. I think he knows his goose is cooked."

"Yeah, I caught all that, but forgive me if I don't feel sorry for him. He threatened you, Webber. We both heard him," Tristan reminded him, looking at Sophie who was nodding.

"I know, but he's just scared," Webber said. "I'm sure they were just empty threats."

"Either way," Tristan concluded, "we need to tell the SEC all about this little visit when we see them tomorrow."

"I will," Webber promised. "Now, Sophie, if you'll excuse us, Tristan's going to help me write my resignation letter."

Sophie's eyes got wide as saucers. "Your resignation letter? You're leaving Kincaid?"

"Yep," Webber acknowledged. "Now that I have someone to share my life with, Tristan and I are going to travel for a while and then decide what we're going to do with the rest of our lives."

Sophie smiled and nodded. "Oh, thank goodness." She turned and started for the kitchen. She stopped and looked over her shoulder. "I always thought that company was going to kill you, but now thanks to Tristan, I can sleep a whole lot better."

Webber smiled. "She's right, you know."

Tristan didn't look happy, and without acknowledging his anger, he turned Webber by the shoulders, marched him into the study, and closed the door behind them.

"Webber James Kincaid," Tristan warned.

"Wait a minute," Webber said, resting both hands on Tristan's shoulders, his lips curving into a half smile. "I must really be in trouble if you're using my full name."

Tristan held his gaze, obviously not joking. "Webber. James. Kincaid," he said in slow, deliberate words. "This is not how our relationship is going to go."

"What's not how our relationship is going to go?" Webber asked, feeling a little confused.

"I would never dream of telling you, nor will I allow you to tell me, that something is not up for discussion."

With that Webber knew immediately to what he was referring. "But, Tris—"

Tristan held up both hands. "Don't 'but, Tris' me. Webber. I'm serious here."

Webber held his ground. "Look, Tristan, I didn't know what frame of mind Nathan was in, and I didn't want you to get hurt."

Webber watched as Tristan clenched his fists together and looked up at the ceiling, obviously choosing his words. "So what you're telling me is that it's okay for me to watch you possibly get hurt, but not the other way around? Is that it?"

"Yes! I mean no!" Webber yelled. "Damn it, Tristan, I couldn't bear it if something happened to you, and I won't promise you that I won't try to protect you again."

Tristan sighed and rubbed at the tears forming in the backs of his eyes. "Webber, just two days ago we agreed we were in this together, for better or for worse and all that crap, and the first chance you have to keep up your end of the bargain, you push me aside and tell me it's not up for discussion."

Webber knew Tristan had him, no matter what the reasons were. He lowered his head. "Damn it," he cursed in defeat. "Okay, you're right. I'm sorry."

Tristan stepped up and took Webber's hand in his. He slid the fingers of his other hand under Webber's chin and lifted his head. "Look, I'm not saying that dealing with Nathan alone wasn't the best thing to do, but damn it, I want a say in the decision. You can't treat me like a weak little boy. I can take care of myself."

Webber took Tristan's other hand. "Okay, okay, I get it now," he said. "But you have to know I would never think of you as weak. Tristan, you're going to be my husband, and I did what comes naturally. I tried to protect you."

Tristan's features softened, but he held on to Webber's hand firmly. "I know that, Web, but you can't make decisions that affect me without my input. The last time that happened, someone I loved decided to get engaged to a woman and didn't think I needed to know."

As if Tristan hadn't already driven his point home, that statement said it all, and Webber finally saw the light.

Webber closed his eyes and nodded. He pressed his lips against Tristan's and whispered, "I'm sorry. Tris, I understand and I'm sorry. It won't happen again."

Tristan leaned into the kiss and Webber deepened it. He ran his tongue along Tristan's bottom lip, nipping as he went. Tristan opened for him, and Webber slipped his tongue in to savor the inside of Tristan's mouth. Webber cupped the back of Tristan's head and was about to back him up against his desk and take him on the spot when there was a knock on the door. "Damn," he whispered against Tristan lips.

Webber stole one last kiss before he answered the door. Sophie must have noticed Webber's flush and slightly swollen lips because she actually blushed when she saw him. "Oh, Mr. Kincaid." She hesitated, looking embarrassed. "I'm so sorry to bother you. I just wanted to know if I should serve dinner before I leave, or if you'd rather I put everything in the oven."

Webber looked at Tristan for some sort of guidance. "Are you getting hungry?"

"Not really," Tristan admitted. "I would like to get a good workout and a shower before dinner. Is that alright?"

Webber looked at Sophie and smiled. "You heard what the man said. I guess dinner goes in the oven."

"Thank you. I'm sorry to have bothered you."

Webber took her in his arms and gave her a squeeze. "You are never a bother."

She seemed to relax in his embrace. "Thanks, Webber," she whispered.

Webber pulled back but kept both hands on her shoulders. He opened his mouth to speak, but thought better of it. He simply smiled.

Sophie winked at him as she turned and headed back to the kitchen.

Webber watched her go and looked at Tristan, shaking his head. "This has to be your doing. What did you say to her?"

"My doing?" Tristan taunted.

"Yes, your doing," Webber repeated. "I've been trying to get her to call me Webber for as many years as I can remember, and all of a sudden you move in and bam, she suddenly knows my first name!"

Tristan smiled coyly. "We may have had a conversation about it, but it was all her decision."

Webber slapped his hands together. "I knew it," he said teasingly. He grabbed Tristan by the forearm and pulled him close, draping his arms loosely over Tristan's shoulders. "Now where were we?" he murmured into Tristan's ear.

Tristan bent his knees, sliding out of Webber's arms, and headed for the door. "Just about to change so we can work out, remember?"

"Why, you little Houdini!" Webber yelled, chasing after him. When they reached the bedroom, Webber took a flying leap and tackled Tristan with both of them landing on the bed laughing hysterically. Over their weeks of lovemaking, Webber had found each and every ticklish spot on Tristan's body, and now he attacked them one by one until Tristan was left in a crumpled ball of human flesh in the middle of the bed begging him to stop.

"Will you even think about trying to slip out of my arms again?" Webber asked, his fingers moving quickly and lightly over Tristan's midsection.

"No!" Tristan yelled through sounds that could only be described as Anderson Cooper manly giggles. "Please stop, I promise I'll never try and escape again."

Webber finally let up and was now on his hands and knees hovering above Tristan with one hand on each side of Tristan's head, staring down at him.

Tristan stretched out beneath him and sighed deeply. "Sucker," he said as he quickly wrapped his arms around Webber's waist, pushed him to his side, and was on top of him so fast Webber didn't know what hit him. He pinned Webber's hands over his head and flashed a sinister smile. "Who's calling the shots now?" he guffawed proudly.

"Okay! Okay, I give," Webber conceded. "Boy, I need to make sure I stay on your good side too. Between you and Sophie, I don't stand a chance."

"You do that," Tristan warned. "And you're right. Sophie and me, we're an unbeatable pair. Now are you going to work out with me or not?"

Webber looked up and raised his eyebrows, trying to make Tristan think he was considering the offer. He finally said, "I'd rather stay right here and work out in a different way, but since that offer's not on the table, I guess I'll take what I can get. But after dinner, I need to get that resignation letter written. Will you help me?"

"Of course I will," Tristan promised. "And after that, I've got plans for you," he offered with a wink. "So we best get a move on."

Webber took Tristan's face in his hands, pulled it down until their lips met, and kissed him deeply. When the kiss ended, Webber whispered, "I can hardly wait."

WEBBER and Tristan touched down at Washington Dulles right on time. Because of security issues, the car wasn't allowed to drive onto the tarmac, so the gate agent grabbed their bags and walked them to the gate where their driver was waiting for them. The driver escorted them through a maze of corridors to the awaiting car and loaded their bags into the sedan. Tristan couldn't remember when he'd last been so nervous, and it didn't help that Webber seemed wound up; Tristan was starting to worry he might explode. From the moment they'd woken up that morning, Webber had seemed very tense and extremely quiet. Webber Kincaid was not a man who rattled easily, so Tristan figured he must really be worried about this hearing, and that in itself was very unnerving.

When they were finally on the road, Tristan noticed that Webber was staring out the window, seemingly deep in thought. He slipped his hand into Webber's and squeezed. Webber returned the gesture and looked at Tristan, smiling weakly before turning his gaze back to the window.

Tristan knew he had to put all his fears aside and be strong for Webber. As scared as he was, Webber needed him, and by God he wasn't going to let him down.

"Web, look at me," Tristan said in a low, hopefully buoyant tone. Webber again turned his head to look at Tristan.

"You didn't do anything wrong," Tristan reminded him with all the confidence he could muster. He kept his voice very low so that only Webber could hear him. "And the SEC and the Department of Justice, if they haven't already, will figure that out very quickly."

"And if they don't?" Webber asked with a worried look on his face.

Tristan squeezed Webber's hand. "Then we fight harder than we've ever fought before," he whispered with conviction. "You contacted the authorities, remember? You could have very easily put a halt to the second acquisition, fired Nathan, and covered up what you knew, and no one would be any wiser, but you didn't. That's got to mean something."

"I sure hope so," Webber admitted.

"Web, I have faith in you and our judicial system. We have the truth on our side, and we've got to hold on to that."

"I love you," Webber said as he leaned in and kissed Tristan lightly.

"I love you more," Tristan said against his lips. "We're gonna get through this together."

As THE car passed Union Station, Webber's heart began to race. He tightened his grip on Tristan's hand and took long, slow breaths to try and regulate his heartbeat. The sedan turned onto F Street and pulled up in front of the building. *I've got to get it together. Tristan's right, I've done nothing wrong.*

Webber released Tristan's hand and got out of the car. He watched silently as Tristan said something to the driver and took what looked like a business card and slipped it inside the pocket of his suit coat. He slid across the seat, stepped out, and closed the door. They entered the building and were directed to security where they took off their shoes, emptied their pockets, and walked through a metal detector. They approached the desk, and Webber told them they were here to see Commissioner Daniel Gallagher. The guard made a phone call and then asked them to have a seat and their escort could be with them momentarily. They were silent, sitting side by side, Webber's shoulders and thighs touching Tristan's, trying to gather as much comfort and strength from his lover as possible.

Ten minutes later they were escorted to the tenth floor and shown to a small conference room with a table, six chairs, a video camera, and a teleconference unit. A camera attendant was already standing behind the camera, but before anyone could make introductions, the commissioner joined them. He looked back and forth between Tristan and Webber and then focused on Webber. "Mr. Kincaid, I'm Dan Gallagher," the commissioner said. "I recognize you from television."

Webber smiled shyly. "Webber Kincaid," he said, offering his hand. "This is my fiancé and former chief administrative assistant, Tristan Moreau."

To the commissioner's credit, he didn't blink an eye at the "fiancé" admission. "Ah, Mr. Moreau, pleased to meet you," he said. The two men shook hands. "You were also on my list of people to question, so I'm glad you're here."

Tristan nodded and swallowed hard, trying to maintain his composure. The SEC scared the hell out of him, but he wasn't going to let Commissioner Gallagher or Webber know that. "Sure. Anything I can do to help the investigation."

Webber cringed inwardly at the thought of Tristan being implicated in any way, but since the SEC knew from the recording between him and Nathan that Tristan was the one who first discovered the discrepancy, there was really no way around it. He cursed himself for mentioning that to Nathan, but he knew if the SEC really wanted to go after Tristan, they would. Maybe it was best that Tristan talked to them now and got it over with.

"Before we get started," Gallagher said, "I'd like you to meet our camera attendant, Sharon Williams. Sharon will be with us for the duration of our meeting."

"If it's alright with you, I'd like to have my attorney conferenced in and have a word with him in private before we get started," Webber said.

"Sure. Sharon and I will just step out and give you a few minutes," the commissioner offered.

"Thank you. Do I need to dial nine or have an access code?" Webber asked before they left. Sharon walked up to the conference unit and dialed in a four-digit code.

"All set," she said. "Just dial your number."

When he reached his attorney, he informed him that Tristan was there with him and that the commissioner wanted to question him as well, so now he was representing them both. His attorney agreed, and Webber opened the door to let the commissioner know they were ready. "My attorney's standing by."

"Perfect. Please have a seat, gentlemen," Commissioner Gallagher offered.

The commissioner shuffled some papers around and began. "This is an informal hearing of the Securities and Exchange Commission regarding fraudulent activities by Kincaid International Corporation or its representatives, a corporation headquartered in Atlanta, Georgia and trading as KIC on the New York Stock Exchange. This hearing is being videotaped and will be admitted into evidence should the SEC determine that Webber James Kincaid or—" He shuffled more papers. "—Tristan Paul Moreau should be brought up on charges regarding this investigation."

The commissioner then looked at Webber. "Mr. Kincaid, please raise your right hand and repeat after me."

Webber did as he was told. "Webber James Kincaid, do you swear to tell the truth, the whole truth, and nothing but the truth, so help you God?"

"I do," he answered.

Commissioner Gallagher turned to Tristan. "Mr. Moreau, please raise your right hand and repeat after me."

Tristan raised his right hand. "Tristan Paul Moreau, do you swear to tell the truth, the whole truth, and nothing but the truth, so help you God?"

"I do," Tristan said.

"The parties have been sworn in and this informal hearing will begin. Mr. Kincaid, your attorney has already provided us with a signed affidavit acknowledging that you had no prior knowledge of any fraudulent activities surrounding the acquisition and divestiture of Marquis Advertising?"

"That is correct," Webber answered.

"I'm here to inform you that Nathan Bridges, your former chief financial officer, has stated under oath that you were not only aware of the false inflation of the sale price for Marquis Advertising, but that you also shared in the proceeds from the transaction," the commissioner said.

"That is a false statement," Webber stated. "In fact, Mr. Bridges came to my home just yesterday and asked me to testify on his behalf, and when I refused, he threatened to implicate me in the transaction. Little did I know he'd already done so. In addition, I have two witnesses who were both present who can testify to the conversation: Mr. Moreau and Mrs. Sophie Wallace, my housekeeper."

"Actually, that would substantiate our findings," Commissioner Gallagher confirmed.

Webber was suddenly confused. "How so?" he asked.

"We were able to trace a large sum of money wired to a bank account in the Cayman Islands belonging to Mr. Nathan John Bridges one day after the acquisition was recorded."

"Very interesting," Webber said. "And…?"

"We were also able to trace the same amount to a Swiss Bank account in the name of Mr. Francois Marquis around the same time."

Webber looked at Tristan and smiled. "I'll be damned."

He turned back to Gallagher. "But I don't understand. How does that information substantiate your findings?"

"Well," Gallagher said. "We were not able to find any large sums either transferred into or out of any of your bank accounts in or around the same time. And the only way we wouldn't know about something of that nature is if you stuffed the money in a coffee can and buried it in your backyard," he said with a weak smile.

"Be my guest," Webber said. "You can dig up our backyard if you like, but I guarantee that you wouldn't find anything there."

The commissioner sighed. "Mr. Kincaid," he continued. "We are well aware of your financial situation and we know that a few million dollars here or there will not make a big difference in your lifestyle. We've also investigated your holdings and know you have no debt, you don't gamble on a regular basis, you don't have a drug problem, and you were not being blackmailed by a scorned lover, which is the motivation for ninety-nine percent of all white collar crimes."

Webber looked at Tristan again. "Aren't you glad to hear all that?" he teased.

Tristan gave him a weak smile, obviously still very nervous.

"Furthermore," the commissioner said, "we've interrogated Mr. Marquis at length, and of course, he denied all charges against him until we offered him a plea deal, and then he suddenly started talking."

"And…?" Webber asked.

"He told us that Mr. Bridges approached him shortly after KIC decided to consider acquiring his company, and that, to the best of his knowledge, you knew nothing about the proposition and the money was split solely between him and Mr. Bridges."

Webber relaxed a little and took Tristan's hand under the table. "So what are you actually telling us?"

"For starters," Commissioner Gallagher said, "we now concur with Mr. Marquis and believe that you had no knowledge of Mr. Bridges's fraudulent activities, and we will not actively pursue an indictment against you. However, the investigation is still ongoing, and if anything turns up contrary to our beliefs, we will look into whatever that is very heavily."

"So you're basically clearing me of any wrongdoing?" Webber asked.

"For now," the commissioner said. "Mr. Moreau, I have a few questions for you and you gentlemen can be on your way."

Tristan sat up straighter, linked his fingers together, and rested his elbows and forearms on the table in front of him, trying not to look as terrified as he was. "Okay," he said.

"I'd like you to tell me exactly how you discovered the discrepancies in the first place."

"Okay," Tristan said.

He explained that shortly after he'd joined KIC, he'd shown an interest in business development, so Webber had given him a few completed acquisition files to review and Marquis had been one of them. And later, while they were on a business trip to evaluate fifteen more possible acquisitions, Moniker's financials and client list seemed very familiar to him, so he brought it to Webber's attention. Webber investigated and that's when they discovered what Nathan had done.

"Would it be normal to recognize financials and client lists from a company you reviewed over a year ago?" the commissioner asked.

"Maybe not for someone who does this as their regular job and looks at numbers all the time," Tristan responded confidently. "But for someone like me just starting out, yeah, I think it would be normal. I mean, I only looked at a few acquisition files, and I studied them over and over again."

The commissioner nodded. "I guess that makes sense. And do you believe that Mr. Kincaid, and remember you are under oath, had any knowledge of this fraudulent transaction?"

Tristan looked at Webber and said with all the conviction he could muster, "Absolutely not; he had a lot of knowledge regarding the transaction, just not the fraudulent part."

The commissioner looked down at his notes. "One more question. Did you ever work directly for or closely with Mr. Bridges?"

"Shortly after I joined KIC, Nathan, I mean, Mr. Bridges offered me a management position within the Finance department."

"And…?" the commissioner asked.

Tristan tried to think quickly on his feet. "For personal reasons, I turned him down flat."

The commissioner gave him a questioning look. "So let me get this straight. You want me to believe that a young man working as an administrative assistant was offered a management position in another department, and he turned it down flat?"

"That's what I'm telling you."

"Can you elaborate on 'personal reasons'?"

"For starters," Tristan explained, "I would never work in the Finance department, and in addition, I'd already started to develop strong feelings for Mr. Kincaid and I didn't want to leave him."

The commissioner flipped through his notes again. "I guess that will be all for now, gentlemen," he stated, looking at the video camera. "This will conclude this hearing.

"Thank you, Sharon, that will be all," the commissioner said. "Would you mind calling a guard to escort Mr. Moreau and Mr. Kincaid back down to the lobby?"

"Sure," she responded as she picked up the phone.

Webber said goodbye to his attorney with the promise of a follow-up call, and he and Tristan stood. He watched as Tristan stepped to the corner of the room and dug a card out of his inside pocket, obviously calling the driver to let him know they were ready. He immediately felt the distance between them, as Tristan hadn't left his side since they'd taken off this morning. He realized for the umpteenth time that he was the luckiest man alive and couldn't help smiling at his soon-to-be husband as he quietly talked on the phone.

The commissioner cleared his throat, which brought Webber out of his trance. "I'd like to thank you for taking the time to meet with me. I'll keep you informed as our investigation progresses, but I can tell you that from everything we've learned so far, I believe Mr. Bridges will be indicted very soon. Oh, and in the spirit of communication, I'll tell you that I will share our findings with the Department of Justice. They are conducting their own independent investigation, of course, but hopefully our information will save them some time and manpower."

Webber again glanced over at Tristan, who was just ending the call. He looked back at the commissioner and extended his hand. "I'm not quite sure how to respond to Nathan's indictment, but thank you for telling me and thank you again for everything. You know how to reach me if you need me."

Tristan joined him and Webber placed his hand on the small of Tristan's back and guided him out of the conference room. Neither one of them said a word until they were safely in the back of the sedan. Webber turned to Tristan, who was facing forward but already smiling broadly. He looked down at their hands linked tightly together and couldn't help but match the smile. "Well?" he said. "Looks like we're one step closer to having this behind us."

Tristan squeezed his hand just a little tighter. "Looks like," Tristan added. "God, I wish we were home so I could crawl into your lap and give you a proper congratulations."

Webber slipped his arm discretely around Tristan's back and whispered into his ear. "Hold that thought, because in a few hours we'll be on Martha's Vineyard, and you can congratulate me all you want. But Tris, remember, don't get too carried away. I'm not off the hook yet."

Tristan threw him a questioning glance. "But I thought—"

"Tris," Webber interrupted. "The commissioner shared what the SEC'd found so far, but until he concludes his investigation, I'm not totally in the clear," he reminded him sadly. "And don't forget about the Department of Justice. All we know is that they're doing their own independent investigation. They haven't even interviewed me yet, and we have no idea how that's going to go."

"Well?" Tristan said drawing out the word. "So far we've had nothing but good news, first from KIC's Board of Directors yesterday and today from the SEC. So I think I'm going to hold on to that until I hear otherwise."

"Good idea," Webber agreed. "I'll do the same."

Three

THE sedan dropped Webber and Tristan off at the terminal for private travelers, where the gate attendant took their bags and walked them to security, their gate, and ultimately their plane. No matter how many times Tristan had flown on a private jet, he was still stunned at how amazing it was and resisted the urge to pinch himself to make sure he wasn't dreaming.

He and Webber made themselves comfortable on the couch, making sure some part of their body was subtly against the other's, which had quickly become a habit when they were in public. The copilot offered them drinks, and before long, the small jet was taxiing to the end of the runway with the two of them sipping scotch.

Tristan suppressed a shiver when Webber's blue eyes found his. He raised his glass in a toast and Tristan smiled as their glasses touched. Tristan was suddenly mesmerized by the glass in Webber's hand. He was unable to draw his eyes away from the long fingers caressing the glass, wiping at the condensation forming there. Tristan's trance was interrupted by the copilot closing the curtain between the cockpit and the cabin, and he was no longer able to control himself—he made his move. He leaned in and pressed his lips against Webber's for a long, drawn-out kiss, keeping one eye on the cockpit while savoring the taste of his lover. "That's part of the congratulations I promised you," he whispered against Webber's lips when the kiss ended. "I'll give you the rest when we're alone."

Webber smiled. "I can hardly wait."

The small plane's engines began to whine as they barreled down the runway. Once they were in the air, Tristan unbuckled his seatbelt and dug through his bag for his iPad. "Let's see if we can find some information on Martha's Vineyard."

"Good idea," Webber agreed.

Tristan did a Google search and started reading little snippets from various websites. He read aloud to Webber. "According to multiple sites, Martha's Vineyard, just south of Cape Cod, is known for being an affluent summer getaway. Often called just 'The Vineyard', the island has a land area of eighty-seven-and-a-half square miles and is the third largest island on the East Coast of the United States."

"Does it say anything about the history?" Webber asked.

"Let me see what I can find," Tristan said as he tapped his iPad a few more times, perusing various sites. "Here we go," he said as he continued reading. "This site says the first explorer to leave any real account of the island was Bartholomew Gosnold. He landed on the cape first, which he named Cape Cod from the abundance of codfish. Then he sailed southward and landed on a small island about six miles southeast of Gay Head. He named this small island Martha's Vineyard. The next day he landed on the larger island, and after exploring it and finding luxuriant grape vines, many beautiful ponds and springs, he transferred the name and called it Martha's Vineyard, in honor of his mother, whose name was Martha."

"Pretty cool," Webber said as he sipped his scotch. "I can't wait to get there."

"Me too," Tristan agreed. "From the pictures on this site, it looks exceptionally beautiful. How much longer before we land?"

As if he'd read Tristan's mind, the copilot pulled the curtain back and gave them the twenty-minute warning. He also told them the views were spectacular as they approached the island. Tristan and Webber turned and kneeled side by side on the couch and looked out of the small round windows. Tristan's mind wandered back to when they'd done the same thing on the way to the Caribbean and how so much had changed between them in such a short time. As they stared out of the windows, they realized the copilot hadn't embellished. The views were indeed spectacular. The late afternoon sun was glistening off of the beautiful emerald-green water with an incredible backdrop of bright blue sky. They passed over a string of islands that, based on the history they'd just read, could only be the Elizabeth Islands. They crossed another body of water that Tristan figured was Vineyard Sound, and then as the plane dipped and turned to the east, the island rose out of the water like a lush green rainforest. They were flying fairly low on the approach to the airport, and Tristan could see summer mansions dotting the coastline with their silver weathered shingles and wraparound porches.

"Look over there," Webber pointed out. "Two lighthouses on either side of that body of water."

The copilot stuck his head out from behind the curtain. "That's East Chop and West Chop, marking the entrance to Vineyard Haven Harbor."

Tristan did a double take. "Thanks for the info, man, but shouldn't you be flying the plane?"

"That's what the pilot's for," he teased as he closed the curtain again.

The plane took a more southeasterly turn, and they saw beautiful white beaches and brightly colored cliffs hanging over the water's edge. As they headed more inland on their final approach, they saw acres and acres of what looked like agricultural farmland. The copilot asked them to secure their seatbelts for landing, and within minutes the plane touched down at the tiny airport and taxied to the gate.

Once out of the plane and standing on the small tarmac, Tristan raised his face to a bright and sunny spring afternoon. Head back and nose tipped upward, he picked up a light breeze carrying a hint of clean and crisp salt air.

"This place is magical. I feel great already. It's amazing how much cooler it is here versus Atlanta and even DC," Tristan commented.

"As much as I love the Caribbean," Webber said, "I could get used to the weather here. It's so brisk, and there's no humidity today."

"Let's get our things," Tristan urged. "I'm dying to get to the inn."

The gate attendant carried their bags to the cabstand, where Tristan hired a taxi to take them to the inn. The cab drove out of the airport and pulled onto a road that could have been anywhere in Middle America. But within minutes, the road turned into a tree-covered lane with ponds scattered here and there, farm stands with fresh fruits and vegetables, and boutique shops and specialty businesses such as pottery shops and glass blowing.

"This is like stepping back in time," Webber said, his head turning from side to side, taking it all in.

"We've got to remember to come back to some of these places," Tristan added.

After a few miles, the cab turned onto a narrow two-lane road where more ponds and small businesses lined the street. Within minutes, Tristan spotted the maroon and gold leaf sign indicating the entrance to the inn. The driver turned onto a single-lane road that wound through natural woodlands for about a half mile, finally ending at a wonderful old farmhouse and well-manicured gardens, all surrounded by waist-high rock walls. When the cab stopped, Tristan paid the driver and they got out and stood in the parking lot, taking in their surroundings.

Tristan caught movement out of the corner of his eye as the front door to the farmhouse opened slowly. A guy came out on to the porch and stopped, apparently sizing them up. After a second, he smiled broadly and walked down the steps to greet them. "Welcome to the Inn at Lambert's Cove; I'm Cavan Winters. My partner and I own this joint," he said with an outstretched hand.

The men exchanged handshakes and greetings. "Nice to meet you, Kevin," Webber said with Tristan nodding in agreement.

The man smiled again. "Actually, it's not Kevin, its Cavan, short for Cavanaugh."

"Oh, sorry," Webber said apologetically.

Cavan waved his hand. "No worries, it happens all the time. Right this way," he said as he picked up their bags and showed them to the front door.

From the moment he stepped inside, Tristan saw that the inn was just as the photos and description had portrayed. The foyer and surrounding rooms were decorated in what could only be considered English Country style. It was warm and inviting. To the left was a large parlor done in red, furnished with deep mahogany leather couches and warm red and gold plaid wingback chairs positioned in front of a large fireplace. To the right was a more formal room decorated in royal blue and greens with yet another massive fireplace. Tristan immediately pictured himself and Webber sprawled across that couch with a good book and a scotch in front of a roaring fire. He imagined the wind howling and a foot of snow on the ground and not having a care in the world while being safe and secure with the man he loved. He was snapped out of his daydream as another gentleman joined them.

Cavan slapped him on the back and introduced him. "Please meet my partner, Sam West. We've owned this place since 2005."

"It's really nice to meet you guys," Sam offered. "Welcome to the Inn at Lambert's Cove."

Webber shook Sam's hand. "Thanks, it's great to be here."

Tristan repeated the gesture. "You have a spectacular place tucked away out here," he assured them.

"Thanks, we think so," Sam replied. "Cavan tells me you guys are here for a wedding tour."

"And for the night," Webber added.

Sam gestured to the front desk. "Great. Let's get you checked in and I'll show you to your room so you can get settled. Then we'll give you the two-buck tour."

"Perfect," Webber said. "What do you need from me?"

"Nothing but a credit card and we're all set."

"I think I put that on my card," Tristan admitted as he dug through his wallet. "Here it is."

Sam tapped a few keys on the computer as he checked them in. "I see you're in the Seaside Room, which is one of our two honeymoon suites. It overlooks the gardens and gazebo of the east lawn. It's one of my favorites."

Tristan looked at Webber then smiled. "Sounds great," he said with a wink.

"Alrighty then, you're all set," Sam said, looking up. "Cavan, do you want to escort these gentlemen to the Seaside Room?"

"It'll be my pleasure," Cavan said, again reaching for their bags. "Oh, and here's our welcome packet, which provides information about our complimentary breakfast and all the other amenities we have to offer during your stay."

Tristan took the welcome packet as they followed one of their hosts up the main stairs. When they reached the landing, a beautiful second floor foyer lined with built-in bookcases opened up to them. There was a leather-inlaid ball-and-claw antique desk, drum table, and a couple of side chairs, along with a computer and printer.

"This is our concierge area," Cavan explained. "Feel free to check email, surf the Internet, print boarding passes, or anything else you need to do anytime. Or if you have your own computer or iPad, we also have Wi-Fi throughout the property."

"Thanks," Tristan answered.

Cavan slipped the key into the lock and pushed the door open. "Here we are, boys, your home away from home, for tonight at least."

Tristan stepped into the room first and was amazed at what he saw. It was what he would consider a quintessential New England-style room. The ceiling was a little lower than usual, and the room was painted in a warm coppery color with a muted tan and cream-colored striped fabric accented with a cream-colored damask. There was a four-poster bed with a canopy attached to a large ceiling medallion over the center of the bed gently cascading to each bedpost and draping to the floor, puddling at the base. There was a skirted table with two houndstooth plaid oversized wingback chairs and a large antique dresser opposite the bed. At the far end of the room was a bathroom with a deep soaking tub, and directly across was a walk-in closet.

"This is beautiful," Webber said, taking it all in.

"Glad you like it. If you get married here, we'll save the other honeymoon suite for your wedding night," Cavan said with a wink.

"I don't know about you, Tristan, but I don't think 'if' is the appropriate word. More like when we get married here."

Tristan smiled and nodded. "My sentiments exactly."

Cavan handed Webber the room key. "I'll let you guys get settled, and when you're ready, come on down and I'll give you the official tour."

"We'll be down shortly," Webber offered.

"No hurry," Cavan said. "Whenever you're ready."

WHEN the door closed behind Cavan, Tristan threw his arms around Webber's neck. "This place is just perfect. I'm so glad John suggested it."

"Me too," Webber said, taking Tristan into his arms and sighing. "I can't wait to be Mr. Webber James Moreau-Kincaid."

Tristan buried his face in Webber's neck. "God, I do love the sound of that."

Tristan felt Webber dip his head and kiss his cheekbone. "What do you say we get the tour over with so we can get back here and practice for our wedding night?"

"You must have read my mind," Tristan teased. "Just give me a couple of minutes to unpack our things and I'll be ready to go."

Webber nodded and Tristan watched him walk over to the window. Tristan slipped out of his suit coat and slid his silk tie off. While he unpacked their overnight bags, Tristan kept an eye on Webber, who was now standing in front of the window seemingly staring into space.

Tristan hurried around the room putting things in drawers, hanging their clothes in the closet, and placing things in the bathroom, always keeping an eye on his fiancé. Webber never moved from his perch. When he was through unpacking, Tristan finally spoke. "Is everything alright, baby?"

Webber must have been very deep in thought because he didn't answer. Tristan walked up behind him and slid his arms around his waist.

Without saying a word, Webber covered Tristan's hands with his own and sighed deeply.

"Web, what's wrong?"

Webber chuckled in a way only he could, a low sexy rumble from deep within his chest. "Nothing's wrong, Tris. I'm fine. I was just thinking that there's beauty all around us. Look at this view."

Webber stepped aside and positioned Tristan in front of the window. Tristan scanned the area outside of their window. Tall trees and hedges surrounded the expansive lawn offering total privacy and seclusion. To the left was a large square lion's head fountain spitting water into a pool from four different directions. To the right was a white octagon-shaped gazebo with a cedar shake roof housing white wicker furniture with overstuffed cushions, obviously for relaxing and watching the day go by.

"It really is beautiful here," Tristan agreed. "But I know there was more on your mind than the beauty."

Webber smiled sheepishly as Tristan turned to him and ran his hands under Webber's coat, caressing his broad shoulders. Tristan slipped the coat off of Webber's shoulders, tossing it onto one of the nearby chairs. He was slowly removing Webber's tie when Webber slipped his arms around Tristan's waist and buried his head in the crook of Tristan's neck. "When did you develop this ability to read me like a book?"

"I've always been able to read you like a book, so answer my question."

Webber sighed but didn't say anything.

They stood there staring at each other, neither one attempting to speak. "Well?" Tristan finally said, cocking his head to one side. "Are you going to tell me what had you so deep in thought?"

Webber cocked his head to the side in a mock gesture and grinned. "Oh, nothing new really," he admitted. "I was just thinking that all of a sudden I have everything I've ever dreamed of, and there's this dark cloud hanging over our heads. I just wish the Department of Justice would conclude their investigation so we can move on with our lives."

Tristan reached down, took Webber's hand, and brought it to his lips, kissing his palm gently then pressing it against his face. "We've received nothing but good news at every turn, and I'm holding on to that, and I think you need to do the same."

"I know," Webber admitted. "I've done nothing wrong, but innocent people sometimes go to jail. I mean, our system works as best as it can, but the fact that people are being released from jail every day because some new evidence presented itself or DNA testing revealed new information proves that the system is flawed. What if, now that I have all I've ever wanted, fate rears its ugly head and that happens to me?"

Tristan frowned. "Come on, stop thinking like that. You've got to stay positive."

Trying to lighten the mood, Tristan quickly added, "Besides, you're too pretty to go to jail." He pressed his lips to Webber's for a quick kiss, but Webber moved his hand up to the back of Tristan's head and held him there for a kiss that ended up being long, deep, and very sensual. When the kiss finally ended, Tristan felt Webber smiling against his lips. "Did you really just say 'too pretty for jail'?"

"Uh oh!" Tristan mumbled. But before he could break free, Webber locked one arm around his waist and started tickling him feverishly with the other. Tristan squirmed and wiggled, attempting to get free, but the more he wiggled, the tighter Webber held on and the more intense the tickling became. Tristan's only option was to lift his feet off of the floor, forcing Webber to hold all of his weight. He figured Webber couldn't keep up the assault while totally supporting him, and he was right. When he felt Webber's arms start to give out from the load, Tristan slid down to the floor and crawled away as fast as he could, scurrying like a rat while howling in laughter and claiming victory. But Webber was quick on his feet. He caught Tristan midway to the bed, flipped him over, and dropped down on top of him. Tristan thought quickly: he faked defeat and when Webber relaxed, Tristan used the element of surprise to roll them both over and settle on top of Webber.

Tristan saw the shocked look in Webber's eyes the moment he realized he'd been outmaneuvered. Webber smiled in surrender. "I love you."

Tristan raised both fists in the air in victory, quite satisfied with himself. "I love you too."

"And thanks for the pep talk," Webber said as he reached down and tried to readjust his obvious erection.

Not ready to give up this intimately playful moment, Tristan straddled Webber's crotch, wiggling in a teasing motion. "You're welcome," he said with a sly grin. He slowly turned the wiggling motion into more of a gyrating grinding and smiled broadly when his efforts produced a look of arousal on Webber's face.

"Keep that up and we'll never get a tour of this place," Webber admitted breathlessly as he gave Tristan's crotch a little squeeze and winked up at him with a playful look.

Tristan shrugged and got to his feet, offering Webber his two hands for a lift. "Okay," he whined. "But we better make it a quick tour."

"Fine by me," Webber agreed as he accepted Tristan's hands and hoisted himself up to his feet. "Let's go check out the wedding venue."

WEBBER and Tristan made their way downstairs and saw Cavan behind the front desk, apparently waiting for them.

"Sorry we're late," Webber offered. Glancing at Tristan with a wicked smile he added, "We got a little distracted by the, uh, beauty of this place."

Cavan cast a knowing glance at both of them and then smiled. "Happens to the best of us," he said. "You guys ready to get started?"

Webber noticed a slight blush creeping up Tristan's chiseled face and he grinned. "We are indeed," he replied, elbowing Tristan.

Tristan slapped him on the arm as Cavan guided them through a room he referred to as the library. The room was an intimate dining room housing seven tables, generously spaced, and lined with floor to ceiling built-in bookcases and several pieces of antique furniture. Webber was immediately taken by the collection of antique leather-bound books. He paused, removing one of the books from the shelf. "I have an antique book collection back in Atlanta," he shared. "This is impressive."

"Thanks," Cavan said proudly. "Most of these came from my mother's estate."

Webber nodded as he saw Tristan admiring an assortment of crystal globes on various types of stands. The light was reflecting off of each globe and casting glimmering rays throughout the room. "Look at these," Tristan said, motioning to Webber. Webber replaced the book and joined Tristan across the room.

"Very cool?" Webber said quizzically, staring at the globes.

"Seriously," Tristan replied.

Out of the corner of his eye, Webber watched as Tristan was already moving on to the next shelf. He followed Tristan's lead and they both stopped when they saw an entire orchestra of antique brass monkeys playing all sorts of instruments, complete with a monkey maestro. Webber heard Tristan chuckle and the sound warmed him to his toes. "I could spend hours in here just looking at everything," Tristan said.

"Feel free," Cavan offered. "But why don't we finish the tour and you guys can come back and stay as long as you like."

Webber looked at Tristan and smiled. "Sounds like a plan," he said.

They continued on and Cavan led them through two large french doors into a ballroom. The room had a solid wall of windows and french doors, all overlooking a magnificent pool and patio area. "Gentlemen, this is the main dining room. The room can accommodate up to seventy-five diners comfortably, eighty if we push it. So if you plan on more than eighty guests, we may need to consider a tented event on the east lawn instead.

"I think we'll be well under eighty," Webber assured him.

Cavan nodded. "It'll be perfect then."

Webber watched as Tristan walked up and down the room admiring the artwork displayed on the walls. "Who is this artist?" he asked, seemingly mesmerized by the collection.

"This is a local artist named Jonathan Ralston," Cavan informed them. "He specializes in architectural art. This particular collection is one of my favorites. Each painting is a very small, but very integral, piece of a much larger structure. You should check out his website."

"We surely will," Tristan replied. "I don't know that much about art, but I love his style."

By now Webber had joined Tristan and together they were studying each painting. "I agree, Tris." He looked over at Cavan. "Are any of these for sale?"

Cavan nodded. "Absolutely. In fact, if you like, I'll have Jonathan come over to meet with you."

"That would be great," Webber said. "Maybe later today or possibly tomorrow morning."

"I'll make a call and see what I can do," Cavan assured him. "So what do you think of the room?"

"I think it's lovely," Tristan said, glancing around. "Webber?"

"Very nice," Webber said, taking Tristan's hand and leading him across the room. When they reached the back wall, they were both smiling from ear to ear. Cavan stepped in front of them and opened french doors that led onto a terrace looking over the expansive pool area with curved stairs leading down to the patio. The entire area was as secluded and private as the area they observed earlier from their room. The kidney-shaped pool, complete with a stone waterfall spilling into the deep end, was surrounded by bluestone and dotted with teak furniture accented by bright red and khaki striped furniture cushions. There were various teak tables with large coordinating patio umbrellas and a large round bluestone hot tub privately tucked away in the corner.

"Stunning," Webber said.

"This is typically where everyone gathers right after the ceremony for cocktails and passed hors d'oeuvres. But if you'd prefer something a little more intimate, the property is very flexible and can be configured in many different ways."

"No," Tristan said, looking at Webber. "I think this will work perfectly, don't you?"

"Absolutely," Webber agreed.

Cavan held up his hand and motioned to the stairs. "Let's go out this way and I'll take you down to the formal wedding garden."

Webber put his hand on the small of Tristan's back and guided him in Cavan's direction. They walked down the stairs to the pool area, around the building, and through a black wrought-iron gate. When Cavan stopped, they were at the entrance to the most magical garden Webber had ever seen. Tristan must have shared his sentiment because he let out a sound that was something between a gasp and a whimper, and Webber felt Tristan reach for his hand and squeeze.

Webber took it all in, admiring the formal English garden and all its beauty. He gauged the rectangle-shaped garden to be approximately seventy-five feet wide by one hundred feet long. There were two perennial gardens about five feet in width each running down the length of the garden, with six feet of well-manicured lawn in the middle forming a natural aisle. On the outside of each perennial garden was another thirty feet of lawn Webber assumed was for seating. Ten-foot-high evergreens trimmed into a formal hedge surrounded the entire garden, giving the large area a warm and cozy feel. A white, three-sided pergola covered in wisteria vines stood at the end of the aisle.

Webber raised his nose as he caught a scent of the wisteria floating on the soft salty breeze. "Tris, can you smell that?"

Tristan inhaled deeply and squeezed Webber's hand again. "It smells amazing."

Webber realized the entire experience was suddenly very dreamlike. He stood frozen in place, savoring the sweet scent of the wisteria vine, taking in the beauty of the garden, and holding Tristan's hand for dear life. He starred at the pergola, picturing Tristan standing under there promising to love him forever, and all the emotions he'd bottled up since the SEC and the Justice Department investigations started to flow. He felt tears streaming down his cheeks and was startled when all of a sudden Tristan was standing in front of him wiping the tears away. "Are you okay, baby? What's wrong?"

Cavan stepped away. "I'll give you guys a couple minutes."

"Thanks," Tristan replied, his eyes never leaving Webber's face.

"Webber," Tristan whispered. "Talk to me."

Webber smiled. "I'm such a baby."

He took Tristan into his arms and held him tightly. "I was just picturing you standing under that pergola ready to commit the rest of your life to me and I just lost it. I love you so much."

Webber felt Tristan smile against his neck.

Tristan placed his hands on Webber's shoulders and took a step back, holding him in place while looking into his eyes. "I love you too, Webber Kincaid, and don't you ever forget it." They stood there staring into each other's eyes until they heard Cavan clear his throat from a few feet away.

Webber turned to Cavan and smiled. "Sorry about that. This place is amazing. Where do we sign?"

Cavan smiled broadly. "I'm so glad you like it. Sam and I feel the same way every time we stroll through the gardens, and we pinch ourselves because we get to live here."

Tristan rubbed his arm up and down Webber's forearm. "I'd be black and blue from all the pinch marks if we lived here."

Cavan chuckled as he started leading them back to the office. "I'll draw up the contracts and you can sign them here or take them with you and send them back later. Either way, I'll block out the dates."

"Thanks," Webber said. "We'll sign them now and give you a deposit?"

"Perfect," Cavan said.

They walked back to the main house and Tristan and Webber sat in the Club Room while Cavan and Sam prepared the documents. They all signed the contract and Webber stood. "I think I need a little nap before dinner. You do have us down for dinner, right?"

Cavan gave Sam a questioning look. "You're all set for eight o'clock."

"Good man," Webber said. "We'll see you at eight."

WEBBER again placed his hand on the small of Tristan's back and guided him up the stairs. He was continually amazed at how naturally their relationship had unfolded and how protective he'd become of his fiancé in just a couple of months, especially after the two long years they'd denied their feelings. He was just about to share that with Tristan when his phone rang. He retrieved the ringing device from his pocket and looked at the caller ID. He smiled and turned the phone so Tristan could see the picture of Deanna's smiling face. He slid his finger across the bottom of the screen. "Hey, D."

Deanna chuckled. "I love when you call me that. How are my favorite guys?"

"Oh so it's *guys* now. Not so long ago it was favorite *guy*."

"Oh, Webber Kincaid, you stop being a baby. Where are you?"

"Believe it or not, we're on Martha's Vineyard."

"Oh my God, Webber, I love it there. A girlfriend of mine owns a house in Edgartown, and last summer I spent a couple of weeks with her. It was glorious."

"We just arrived this afternoon, but so far I concur."

"Where are you staying?"

"We're at the Inn at Lambert's Cove and we couldn't be happier. In fact, we signed a contract to get married here in a couple of months."

"Oh Webber, that's fantastic! Where's Tristan? Let me talk to Tristan."

Webber held the phone out. "She wants to talk to you."

Tristan took the phone. "Hey, Doll."

Webber saw the smile start to form at the corners of Tristan's mouth until it became a full-on beam of white teeth.

Tristan's head bobbed up and down as he talked. Webber listened.

"Thanks, Deanna, yeah, we're so happy—"

"I love you too," Tristan said.

It was obvious she wasn't going to let Tristan get a word in. He started answering her apparent questions in rapid succession.

"Yes, of course you are—"

"I sure hope so—"

"Don't I know it—"

Tristan smiled broadly as he handed the phone back to Webber. "She's happy for us." He giggled.

"Obviously," Webber said as he put the phone back to his ear.

"I love him so much, Webber, don't you fuck this up."

"Thanks for the vote of confidence."

"Oh stop it, you know what I mean."

"I'm just teasing. I know I'm the luckiest man in the world, and I will not screw this up," he said to Deanna, looking directly at Tristan.

"Anyway," Webber said. "Enough about us, let's talk about you. How are you and the baby making out?"

"We're doing just fine except for the fact that I'm starting to look like I'm carrying a volleyball under my blouse."

"Are you showing that much already?"

"I'm afraid so, and… the cat is out of the bag."

"Really. Who busted you?"

"*People* magazine ran a picture of me exiting my OBGYN's office with a caption that read 'Is that a baby bump we see under runway model Deanna Lynn's loose-fitting blouse?'"

Webber chuckled.

"It's not funny, Webber. Ever since that photo ran, my publicist has been bombarded with calls trying to confirm the rumors and find out who the baby daddy is. You know they all suspect you."

"I'm so sorry, baby," Webber said, before registering Deanna's words. "Wait! Me?"

He saw Tristan raise an eyebrow and throw him a concerned look. He put his hand over his phone and whispered, "Her pregnancy's out and everyone thinks I'm the father."

Tristan nodded with a slight frown as Webber went back to talking to Deanna. While still listening to Deanna ramble, Webber unlocked their door and stood aside for Tristan to enter their room. He followed and turned to lock the door behind them. When he turned around again, Tristan was standing directly in his path with a wicked look on his face. Webber stared in amazement as Tristan dropped to his knees and slowly bent down to untie Webber's right shoe. He slipped it off his foot and then did the same to the left. He came back up to his knees and unbuckled the belt on Webber's suit pants. He released the fastener and inner button and unzipped the fly. Webber's pants fell to the floor in one quick motion. Tristan slowly lifted Webber's feet one at a time and pushed the pants away.

Webber knew he was stuttering and stammering on the phone, but he couldn't help it, and he knew he was very close to losing control. Thank God Deanna was still rambling and didn't seem to notice his incoherence. But he let out a loud gasp when Tristan placed his mouth over his cotton briefs and started nibbling at Webber's already thickening length.

"Deanna, can I call you back? I… I've got to go."

"Webber, is everything alright?"

Right then Tristan laughed loudly. "Hang up the phone, Web."

Webber tried his best to say goodbye to Deanna normally, but it was virtually impossible.

"What are you two doing?" Deanna asked without thinking. "Oh God, please tell me you're not...." Her voice faded off. "Webber Kincaid, I'm going to slap the hell out of you when I see you. Do you hear me?"

"Uh huh" was all Webber could say, struggling to make his brain function with his mouth. "I'll... uh, I'll call you... later."

Webber pressed the button to end the call just as Tristan peeled his briefs down to his ankles. He moaned and dropped the phone to the floor when Tristan took him into his mouth, the wet heat consuming him from head to toe. He gripped the back of Tristan's head with his left hand and rode the wave of pleasure, feeling his knees weaken further with every one of Tristan's movements. "Oh my God, Tris, you feel amazing."

Tristan continued his onslaught, showing Webber no mercy. "If you don't stop, this is all going to be over before it gets started."

Webber slipped from Tristan's mouth and he watched as Tristan stood up in front of him and looked into his eyes longingly. To Webber, time stood still, and he realized that he'd never felt as wanted as he did in this very second. He relished the realization that Tristan loved and wanted him above everything else.

Tristan placed both hands on Webber's dress shirt and pulled it apart in opposite directions, sending buttons flying across the room and bouncing off whatever was in their path. Webber allowed him to slip the shirt from his shoulders and watched as Tristan tossed it across the room. He crushed his mouth on Webber's in a kiss that was wet, sloppy, and desperate, just the way Webber liked it. One minute Webber felt Tristan's hands running up and down his back frantically, and the next they were running through his hair and down his torso, stopping when they reached his ass. Tristan kneaded and squeezed until he pulled Webber's ass cheeks apart and found what he was after. He broke their kiss just long enough to wet his middle finger and smiled as he covered Webber's lips again.

Webber inhaled abruptly and saw stars when Tristan's middle finger penetrated him, his knees finally giving out from the sheer pleasure. Tristan caught him and supported his weight as he massaged Webber's insides while never breaking their kiss.

Webber savored Tristan's tongue moving in and out of his mouth while one of Tristan's strong arms supported him and the other played at his backside, stroking his insides into a frenzy. Every nerve ending was on fire, and he hungrily gave in to the feelings. His throbbing erection brushed against the inside of Tristan's leg, and he had to fight hard not to explode right then and there. Trying to regain some sense of control over his own body, Webber locked his knees into place and reclaimed the use of his legs. He slowly worked his hands between them and unbuttoned Tristan's shirt. He moved his hands lower until he found Tristan's belt buckle and worked it free and unfastened the clasp, releasing Tristan's pants to hit the floor. He gathered all the strength he could manage, wrapped his arms around Tristan's waist, and lifted him off of the floor to carry him across the room, Tristan's mouth still covering his and his finger still lodged deep inside of him. When they reached the bed, Webber lowered Tristan to his feet and slipped Tristan's shirt over his shoulders. He slowly removed Tristan's hand from inside him and gently shoved him onto the bed. He removed Tristan's shoes and socks and slipped Tristan's pants off and tossed them to the side. He was looking down at the most gorgeous man he'd ever seen in nothing but his underwear. In a shocking move, Tristan raised his middle finger to his nose, apparently savoring Webber's unique scent and then slipped it into his mouth, giving Webber a seductive grin. "I love the way you smell and taste," he whispered.

Webber fought to keep himself under control, doing his best not to lose it. He wasn't through with Tristan in any sense of the word and wanted to make this last for as long as he could. He reached down and hooked his fingers in Tristan's underwear, then ripped them down to his feet, freeing him from the confines of the cotton briefs. "You are the most beautiful man I have ever seen."

Tristan raised his arms up to Webber, but Webber held up one finger. "I'll be right back."

He headed for the bathroom and within seconds was back with a bottle of lubricant and a hand towel. Tristan again reached out to him, and Webber lay down, straddling him and leaning in for another kiss. This kiss was slower, more sensual and less frantic. He savored Tristan's mouth, their tongues exploring while Webber gyrated his hips against Tristan's erection. He ran one hand through Tristan's hair, caressing his soft locks, and used the other to flip open the lubricant. He squeezed a small amount onto his hand and reached around and applied some to himself as well as to Tristan, savoring Tristan's deep guttural moan against his lips in response to his actions. He reached back and positioned Tristan at his opening and slowly lowered himself onto his lover. Webber felt Tristan gasp against his mouth as he impaled himself ever so gently, giving himself adequate time to adjust to the intrusion. Webber gradually felt the sting turn to a tingle and then to pure pleasure. He started to move, gingerly at first, getting used to the sensation. He moved up almost to the point where Tristan would escape him, but just in time, he would carefully ease down until he felt Tristan's pubic hairs tickle the tender skin around his opening. For the second time in minutes, his nerve endings were on fire. The sensation of being full, full with Tristan, was almost more than he could stand. As he moved, he wanted more of Tristan. He sat up, breaking their kiss and leaning back into the motion, taking Tristan as far as he could go. He felt Tristan slowly start to thrust up and back down to meet his strokes, and within seconds they were moving as one. Webber's head was thrown back and his eyes were closed, enjoying the pure ecstasy of his lover. He opened his eyes when he felt something cold and wet and watched as his lover applied lubricant and began to slowly stroke him up and down, matching his thrusts. "I won't last too much longer," Webber whispered, slowly spiraling out of control, his hands behind him bracing his gyrating body as he rode his lover.

"I'm right with you, baby. Let it go; shoot for me, please."

The sensation of his lover deep inside him while Tristan stroked his erection was too much for him to handle. He felt his orgasm building deep within his gut. He savored the feeling as the impending release made its way to his balls and then spilled, the first round hitting Tristan on the chin, the second on his chest, and the third landing on Tristan's tight stomach. Webber roared through his release, not able to control his vocal chords or his emotions. Seconds later, Webber watched Tristan throw his head back as he gripped Webber's thighs, repeatedly thrusting up hard and deep as he hit his peak.

Webber leaned down and covered Tristan's mouth with his own in a gentle but sensual kiss. He felt Tristan smile against his lips, and he pulled back, wondering what was so funny. "What?"

"That was so fucking hot," Tristan said. "When can we do it again?"

Webber laughed as well this time. "I think I'll need a few minutes to recharge my batteries, but soon. I hope."

"Good answer," Tristan replied.

Webber flinched as Tristan slipped out of him, and he suddenly felt very empty and immediately missed Tristan inside him. "I take that back. Let's go again."

"Just like you to call my bluff," Tristan chuckled. "Okay, I need a minute as well."

Webber stretched out next to Tristan and rubbed his fingers in his release. Tristan took his hand and sucked each finger clean. Webber felt himself getting hard instantly. "Keep doing that and I won't need any time after all."

Tristan rolled over to his side, facing Webber, and gently kissed him. "I love you more than I ever thought possible."

"I feel the same way, Tris."

They wrapped their arms around each other, neither wanting to break the connection, and fell asleep almost instantly.

TRISTAN woke a little disoriented. He held on to Webber tightly while he tried to focus on his surroundings. It only took him a few minutes to remember where they were, and once he had, he laid his head back down on the bed, pulling Webber closer to him.

Webber started to stir and Tristan kissed him gently on the tip of his nose. "Hey, sleepy head."

Webber blinked a few times. "What time is it?"

Tristan looked at the clock on the bedside table. "Six thirty."

Webber stretched and snuggled in closer to Tristan, rising up on his elbow. "When is the last time I told you I love you?"

"Oh, I guess a little over an hour ago maybe."

"Damn, that will never do."

Webber laid his head on Tristan's chest, but said nothing.

"Well?" Tristan said in a mock huff.

"Well what?" Webber teased.

"I thought you were going to tell me how much you love me."

"Where would you get that idea?" Webber asked, barely able to control himself.

Tristan sighed. "Oh, never mind."

Webber came back up on his elbow. "I love you, Tristan Moreau."

Tristan turned with a bright smile. "I love you too, Webber Kincaid."

"So," Webber said, gently caressing Tristan's chest. "What do you say we shower, go downstairs and get a glass of wine, and then take another stroll around the gardens?"

"I love that idea," Tristan replied. "We haven't seen the tennis courts, the apple orchard, or the vineyard I read about online."

Webber slapped Tristan's chest, kissed him on the cheek, and jumped out of bed. "Up and at 'm then."

THIRTY minutes later they were strolling through the formal wedding gardens, Webber carrying a glass of wine and an open bottle of Ramey

Chardonnay and Tristan carrying his own glass while his other hand held on to Webber's arm. Tristan took a sip of his wine and savored the rich, buttery flavor on his tongue until he swallowed. He once again took in his surroundings and pictured chairs on both sides of the perennial gardens. They were filled with guests watching him and Webber exchange their vows. Unfortunately, that image made him wonder who from his family would actually show up to support them. But hey, if he and Webber could find their way to one another, a miracle could actually happen, couldn't it?

From the corner of his eye, he saw Webber staring at him. "Penny for your thoughts?"

Tristan sighed, trying to decide how he wanted to proceed. He'd never really shared much about his family with his fiancé although Webber had recently begun to inquire about them. Luckily, something or someone always interrupted their conversation, and he'd been able to casually change the subject. Not that he didn't want Webber to know everything about him, he just didn't know how to explain the situation. He hadn't planned on dropping this particular bomb on him now, but hell, maybe now was as good a time as any.

Tristan downed his wine and let go of Webber's arm, rubbing his own sweaty palm against his slacks. He suddenly had an aching feeling in his stomach, and he was beginning to tremble slightly. He also knew he was fidgeting, but he just couldn't stop it. When he opened his mouth to speak, his shaky voice didn't sound like his own. "I was just thinking about how many of my family members might actually show up to support us."

Tristan wasn't shocked to see the surprised look on Webber's face at the mention of his family. Webber was quiet for a few seconds, apparently trying to choose his words carefully. "And what's the verdict?" he asked softly.

Tristan shrugged. "Hell if I know; can we walk?" he asked, his voice still very shaky. "There are some things I need to explain to you about my family."

"Anything you want, baby," Webber said. "But before we walk I need to do one thing."

Tristan tilted his head to one side wondering what in the hell Webber needed to do right now of all times. Before he could ask, Webber threw his arms around him, still holding his wine glass and the wine bottle, and squeezed him as tightly as his grip would allow. "I just want you to know that I love you and nothing you need to tell me will ever change that, okay?"

Tristan nodded in the crook of Webber's neck, tears threatening to burst from the backs of his eyes. Webber pulled away, putting the wine bottle and his glass in one hand and taking Tristan's hand with the other. "Where to?"

Tristan looked around and stopped when he saw the charming gazebo. "There," he pointed.

"Perfect," Webber agreed.

They walked in silence along a red brick path, hands still linked together tightly. Tristan turned his head from side to side as he took in the surroundings while he tried to calm his nerves. They passed an herb garden tucked away into a corner of the main house on the right, while on the left they approached a black lion's head fountain spitting water into a pool nestled into a glorious wall of lilacs at least eight feet tall. Next, they crossed the front of the inn, walked through a white arbor, passed a koi pond, and sauntered across the lawn, finally stopping when they stepped into the gazebo. Webber released his hand and gestured for him to take a seat on the white wicker loveseat. Tristan sat and watched as Webber poured them each another glass of wine and took a seat next to him. Webber put his free arm around Tristan's back and relaxed against him.

Tristan held up his glass, tapping it against Webber's. "Cheers."

"Cheers," Webber repeated, but said nothing more.

Tristan had just found the courage to speak when Webber nudged him and slowly gestured with his chin in the direction of a row of trees about twenty yards away. Tristan turned to see a mother deer and her fawn feasting on whatever was on the ground below the trees. "That must be the apple orchard," Tristan whispered, careful not to spook the animals. "They're beautiful and so gentle."

"They are," Webber agreed as he kissed Tristan's cheek. "And so are you."

The two men quietly watched until the doe and fawn had had their fill of apples and moved on to their next feeding ground.

Without the calming distraction of the deer, Tristan again felt his stomach start to twist into knots. Out of the corner of his eye, he watched Webber, still silent and sipping on his wine. Tristan knew in his heart Webber was giving him plenty of space and time to find the courage to say whatever it was he needed to say, and he loved him for that.

"Webber, I need to talk to you about my family."

Webber squeezed his shoulder in response. "Okay."

"I... I'm not sure where to start."

"How about if I get you started?" Webber asked, not waiting for a response. "How many siblings do you have?"

"I have two brothers, one older and one younger," Tristan responded.

"I know you moved to Atlanta from New York. Is that where you grew up?"

Tristan couldn't stand it any longer, so he just blurted it out. "Webber, my dad and older brother went to jail, and I helped put them there."

Four

TRISTAN was shocked when Webber didn't pull away. In fact, not only did he not pull away, Webber tightened his hold on him. "I'm sorry for blurting it out."

"No, I'm sorry. Baby, I'm sure you did what you had to do. Do you want to tell me about it?" Webber asked.

"I've always wanted to tell you about it, but I just never knew how."

"Tris, as I said earlier, you must know how I feel about you. Nothing you can say will ever make me feel differently."

Tristan sighed and settled into Webber's embrace, looking out over the orchard as if all the words he needed were hanging from the trees along with the apples. He took another sip of his wine and took a deep breath. "My dad owned a small investment firm on Wall Street. When my older brother graduated from college, he joined the firm and they worked together very closely. My dad's administrative assistant left for maternity leave just as I was finishing my freshman year in college, and because I was majoring in business administration, I agreed to help him out and fill her position on my summer break. That kept him from hiring a temp, helped me get some business experience, and gave me the opportunity to make a little money. It seemed like a good idea at the time."

"Not so good now?" Webber asked.

"You have no idea," Tristan replied.

"Tell me," Webber whispered, kissing him again on the cheek.

"Well, all seemed fine in the beginning. I was learning a lot about business, picking up some pointers on investing, and just gathering all the experience I could. Then some things started to not add up. To make a long story short, my dad and brother were involved in a ponzi scheme, duping their customers out of tons of money."

Webber again kissed his cheek, allowing his lips to linger there a few extra seconds. "And you figured it out and turned them in."

"Part of that statement is true. I did figure it out, but before I could confront my father, the business was raided," Tristan explained. "Apparently, the firm was already under investigation and being watched very closely. When the SEC decided they had enough information, they made their move with the help of my dad's assistant, who had been feeding them information all along."

"I'm so sorry. Tris, that couldn't have been easy for your family. Where was your mother during all of this?"

"Oh hell," Tristan chuckled. "She was too busy being a Manhattan socialite wife and dabbling in her various charities to care what was happening outside of her world."

"So how did it all end?" Webber asked.

"My dad and brother were arrested and indicted. I was subpoenaed and forced to testify against them, and my family never forgave me for it. Our relationship is strained at best, except for my little brother Gage. He is three years younger than me, and they weren't able to turn him against me. Gage is the only one I have any type of relationship with."

"It seems like Gage is the only smart one in the entire bunch," Webber teased. "Do you see your dad and brother in jail?"

"No, they're out now, have been for over a year, but when I tried to contact them, neither wanted anything to do with me."

"And your mother?" Webber asked.

"We talk occasionally, behind my dad's back of course. But I'm not crazy enough to think she'll ever stand up to him and fight for any type of relationship with me."

Webber sighed, sounding a little disappointed. "So that's why you turned Nathan down when he offered you that job in the Finance department."

"Partly," Tristan admitted honestly. "After what I went through with my dad and brother, I'd convinced myself that I had no desire to ever work in any capacity of finance again. But if I'm being totally honest, that wasn't the deciding factor."

Webber raised an eyebrow.

"You were," Tristan murmured.

Webber looked surprised. "Me?"

"Yes, you. You made me start to love it again. Working with you on potential acquisitions made me realize how easily I could get lost in the work and how much I'd missed it. But... what I said about already having feelings for you was the honest to God's truth. I wouldn't have left you even if I had been offered a position as the head of marketing."

Webber put his wine glass down, looking a little relieved, and wrapped his arms around Tristan, holding him tightly. "At first I thought 'personal reasons' meant me. Then you said you'd never work in finance and that sort of threw me, but now it all makes perfect sense. Please don't feel like you have to keep anything from me ever again. I would never judge you or anyone else; I love you."

Still being held tightly by Webber, Tristan gave in to the embrace. "I love you too."

"I'm so sorry this had such an impact on your family, but Tris, your family's demise was not your fault. The only people to blame here are your father and your brother." Webber released Tristan and looked into his eyes. "Not. Your. Fault."

Tristan met Webber's gaze, then looked away. "But regardless of who's to blame, I have no family except Gage."

Webber wrapped Tristan in his arms again and whispered, "We'll just build our own damn family. What do you say to that?"

Tristan felt the tension he'd hadn't realized he'd been carrying simply melt away while wrapped in Webber's arms. "I think that's a great idea."

"We have Kenton, Amani, and Kit, Deanna, Sophie, and Gage. That's enough to start with," Webber exclaimed. "When do I get to meet Gage?"

"Soon, I hope. He's a veterinarian and lives with his partner Andy on their small ranch just outside of Nashville."

"Gage is gay?" Webber asked in a surprised tone.

"Yep. That's probably one of the reasons we stayed close."

"So we add Andy to our list of family members. Look, our family is growing already."

Tristan buried his head in Webber's neck. "God, I love you."

"Ditto," Webber replied.

They talked for a while longer, and before they knew it, the activity level of people arriving for dinner started to increase. Tristan looked down at his watch. "Wow, it's already time for our reservation. You hungry?"

"Starved. And I'm looking so forward to sampling their food. You know, we signed that contract having no idea if their food was even edible."

"Take a look around you, Web," Tristan said. "Do you think these guys would do anything half-ass?"

Webber chuckled. "I guess you're right. Worst case scenario, we hate their food and bring in our own chef."

"I doubt that'll be necessary," Tristan teased. "But good idea nonetheless."

THE restaurant did not disappoint. As they walked toward the main house and restaurant, the sounds of Edith Piaf filled the air, reminding Tristan of a brief trip he'd taken to France. Once inside, Sam and Cavan put them at a lovely secluded table in the corner overlooking the pool area. Webber ordered a vintage bottle of Bourgogne Rouge VV "Maison Dieu" Domaine de Bellene, and their night officially began.

They started with oysters on the half shell, then as an appetizer Webber ordered grilled white peaches with imported prosciutto, shaved red cabbage, and micro greens, and Tristan ordered steamed mussels in caramelized ginger, green onions, and coconut milk. For entrees, Webber had the seared sea scallops and Tristan horseradish-dusted veal.

Sam and Cavan took turns seamlessly stopping by to make sure everything was to their liking, but never lingered long enough to intrude on their privacy. They finished the meals off by sharing a Belgian chocolate molten lava cake and a bottle of Ruffino Moscato d'Asti Italian dessert wine.

Webber wiped the corners of his mouth with his napkin, exhaled, and placed the napkin on the table in front of him. "How stupid was it of me to doubt these guys," Webber insisted. "That was undoubtedly one of the best meals I've ever had."

"Absolutely," Tristan agreed. "What do you say we take another walk before we turn in?"

"Sounds perfect. I don't think I could sleep anyway."

"Who said anything about sleeping," Tristan joshed with a wink.

Webber smiled. "On second thought, I am a little bit tired; maybe we should just turn in."

"Too late," Tristan taunted. "A walk it is."

After saying goodnight to their hosts, Tristan led Webber out of the front door and down the steps to the brick walkway. The place was just as lovely at night as it was during the day. The front porch was adorned with candles of all sizes, and torches romantically lit the front lawn and the walkway to the parking lot. The full moon was high overhead, and the glow alone would have sufficiently lit the walkway, but the raw flames added another element to the beauty. "Let's go this way this time," Tristan said, tugging Webber's arm in a new direction.

Webber smiled broadly as they walked along the path that ran beside a rock wall surrounding the property. Before long they stumbled onto the vineyard Tristan had read about. "Look, Web, it's the vineyard," Tristan said, running up and plucking one of the grapes off of the vine and popping in into his mouth. It wasn't a large vineyard, maybe six or seven vines covering about twenty feet of arbor, but the grapes were sweet and plentiful. Tristan ran back and took Webber by the hand, dragging him under the arbor where they were suddenly surrounded by foliage and grapes. Hundreds of clumps of grapes hung down and Tristan reached up and grabbed a handful. He fed the grapes to Webber one at a time, kissing him in between bites until Webber had his fill and grabbed the bunch out of Tristan's hand and flung them to the side. He took Tristan into his arms and, in a Rhett Butler from *Gone with the Wind*-type move, dipped Tristan over his knee and kissed him feverishly.

When the kiss ended, they were both out of breath, Webber's swollen lips glistening in the filtered moonlight. "Wow, I think I've just been good and kissed," Tristan said, smiling up at Webber. "Do it again."

Webber did as he was told, running his fingers through Tristan's long locks and fighting the urge to strip him right there and have his way with him. But there was something about the anticipation of what would follow when they got back to their room that kept him in check.

"Come on, Web, there's more of the path we haven't explored yet. Can we go?" Webber didn't think he'd ever seen Tristan so lighthearted and free, and he loved this new Tristan. They walked hand in hand along the path until they ran into the tennis court tucked in a secluded spot away from the main hustle and bustle of the inn traffic. They continued following the path until it was about to circle back to the main house when Tristan spotted a well-beaten path leading off into the woods. "Come on, Web, let's see where it goes."

Tristan dragged him along, acting like a bloodhound on a scent. It took a minute for his eyes to adjust to the filtered moonlight, but when they did, he really didn't have any trouble staying on the path. Something seemed to be drawing Tristan forward. Webber didn't know what, but he sure as hell was going to find out. After a few long stretches and a turn or two, the path opened up on the most beautiful pond Webber had ever seen. It was nestled in the middle of hundred foot evergreens, and the water was so clear, you could see the bottom from just the moonlight. "Oh my God, Tristan, look at this."

They were both stunned. Tristan's eyes were the size of saucers as he scanned the scenery before him. "It's beautiful."

Tristan took one more look at Webber and the pond, then started toeing out of his shoes. "Come on."

"What are you doing? Webber asked, already knowing the answer.

"We're going skinny dipping."

"Wait. What if—"

"What if what, Webber?" Tristan asked. "Are we too old to take a chance, have a little fun? What's the worst that can happen, someone asks us to leave? If they do, we put our clothes back on and leave. It's as simple as that."

Before Webber could say a word, Tristan was already naked and unbuttoning Webber's shirt. He slipped the shirt over Webber's shoulders and unbuckled his slacks. "The hell with it," Webber said as he toed off his shoes. "The last one in bottoms tonight."

"Wait!" Tristan teased. "That's no incentive for me to hurry."

They both chuckled. "Good point," Webber agreed.

Tristan grabbed Webber's hand and dragged him to the edge of the pond, their clothes in heaping piles of fabric dotting the shoreline.

"On three," Webber said as he dug his toes into the sandy shore. "One, two, three." They both did a shallow dive and entered the water. Tristan surfaced, immediately turned onto his back, and did the backstroke toward the center of the pond. Webber swam right under Tristan and surfaced behind him and encircled Tristan's chest when he backstroked right into Webber's arms.

Webber turned him around and covered Tristan's lips with his own, both of them treading water in the middle of the pond. They both stopped kicking and slipped below the surface just as they had done in the Caribbean the first time they'd ever kissed. Webber felt his feet hit the sandy bottom and instinctively pushed back up with Tristan following his lead. They broke the surface together and started treading water again.

"This is an oasis," Tristan murmured. "It's totally like a dream. I can't believe we found this place."

"I know," Webber concurred. "As far as I'm concerned, this will always be our special place."

For the next few hours, they swam, played, made love on the shore, and swam and played some more. Long after midnight, they snuck back into the inn, holding their clothes in front of them as they tiptoed up the stairs to their room. Just when they thought they'd made it back unnoticed, they heard Sam laugh from the office below. "Good night, boys."

Surprised and giggling like schoolgirls, they both replied in unison, "Good night."

AFTER an incredible breakfast the next morning, they decided to have a car delivered so they could spend a few hours quickly exploring the island before they left. Armed with a map of the island and an island guide, they loaded their bags into a convertible Mustang, said goodbye to their hosts with a promise to stay in touch, and set out to explore this little slice of heaven.

They followed Cavan's directions and started out heading up-island—really south, but referred to as up-island by the locals because of the higher elevations—passing though little towns like Chilmark and Menemsha.

"I just can't get over how large this island is," Webber said as they passed acres and acres of pastoral land. A few miles later, they rounded a bend on South Road and the scenery opened up with views of small bodies of water on either side of the road with vistas of the Vineyard Sound and Nantucket Sound beyond.

Tristan reached over and took Webber's hand. "If you can find a place to pull over, I'd love to get a picture of this."

Webber slowed down and scanned the road ahead, eventually finding a small spot with what appeared to be a solid shoulder. He checked his rearview mirror and pulled the small car as far off of the road as he could. He put the car in park and leaned over toward Tristan.

The sun was climbing high in the sky and reflecting off of the water, making the small whitecaps glisten like emeralds. "I don't think I've ever seen anything so beautiful," Tristan said as he snapped picture after picture with his iPhone. He quickly turned the iPhone in Webber's direction and got a few shots before Webber put his hand up to stop him.

"Enough of me; we're here for the scenery."

"You are my scenery," Tristan teased. "Anything beyond you is just icing on the cake."

"Smooth talker." Webber chuckled, adding a quick wink before checking his rearview mirror again and pulling back onto the two-lane road.

"I speak only the truth, and you better get used to it," Tristan replied, waving him off.

Their next destination was Aquinnah, formerly known as Gay Head, home of the famous Gay Head cliffs and the Gay Head lighthouse and some of the best views the island had to offer. Reaching the end of the road, they parked and walked up to the overlook. They were now gazing out into the choppy Atlantic Ocean, dotted with lobster boats here and there, the lush green island of Nomans Land to the left and the string of Elizabeth Islands, the famous cliffs, and the Gay Head light to the right. The famous cliffs were a muted palette of reds, coppers, golds, and browns. Webber and Tristan posed as a fellow tourist snapped their picture, and they were off to their next destination.

"What's next?" Webber asked.

"Edgartown," Tristan said, glancing at the island guide. "It was the first town settled on the island."

Forty-five minutes later, they were walking hand in hand up and down the quaint streets of Edgartown, admiring the old captain's houses with their rose-covered trellises and looking up to see widow's walks perched high above the rooflines. "Up there is where captains' wives supposedly spent hour after hour watching for their husbands' ships to return from the sea," Tristan reported. "I hope I never have to do that for you," he added.

"I can hardly picture that." Webber chuckled.

For lunch they dined on french onion soup and fish and chips at a little pub called The News from America that dated back to the eighteen hundreds and was where everyone gathered to get the latest happenings from the mainland.

They next drove along the two-lane road following the state beach, which was about five miles of sandy white beaches connecting the town of Edgartown to the harbor town of Oak Bluffs. In Oak Bluffs, they drove along the breakwater where casual seafood restaurants lined the inner harbor, serving, among others, visitors that came to the Vineyard by private boat or day-trippers that came by ferry.

Before they knew it, it was time to head to the airport. "I still can't believe how big this tiny island is," Tristan shared, looking at the boats lined up in the harbor.

"I know what you mean," Webber confessed. "I'm not sure what I expected, but it certainly wasn't this."

The GPS quickly guided them to the airport, where their aircraft was ready and waiting. Because they were flying privately, there was no need to go through security, so they walked right onto the tarmac and boarded their plane, bags in hand.

THEY took off shortly after boarding, and twenty minutes later they were comfortably seated side by side sipping single-malt scotch. Tristan was staring out of the window, obviously deep in thought.

"Can you keep it down over there?" Webber teased. "You're thinking rather loudly."

Tristan turned and flashed him that million-dollar smile. "Very funny," Tristan murmured. "I was just imaging what our wedding might be like."

Webber took Tristan's hand, brought it to his lips, and kissed his palm. "Whatever you want is perfectly fine with me," he admitted. "Just keep me in the loop so I'll know what to do?"

Tristan glared over at him with the hint of a smile. "Webber Kincaid, you take that back! We're going to plan this entire wedding together, down to every last detail," Tristan said wryly.

"Oh goodie," Webber said sarcastically, releasing Tristan's hand and his seatbelt. "You know planning and coordinating aren't my forte," he warned.

"What! You think I sat around all day long and planned weddings?" Tristan snapped.

Webber chuckled, loving this side of his fiancé. "No, don't get your panties in a wad. I didn't mean it like that." He looked past Tristan and gazed out the window. "It's just… well, to be honest, I'm just the scatterbrained executive that waited for you to get to work every day so you could tell me where I needed to be and what I needed to be doing. And… I kind of liked it that way."

Webber saw a hint of pride appear on Tristan's face. "And I'll always do that for you, but this is our one and only wedding day, and I'd like it to be everything we want it to be."

"Me too," Webber agreed. "So tell me what you have in mind? But… before you answer that, let me just say that as long as you're there, it's perfect for me already."

Tristan smiled warmly and leaned in and kissed Webber's cheek. "I-I don't really know; that's why I was imagining different scenarios. I mean… I never expected to get married, so I never really thought about it."

"Well, if I had my way," Webber teased, taking Tristan's hand again, "I'd like something small and intimate with just a few friends and family."

Tristan seemed to relax a little and looked out the window again.

He released Tristan's hand again and brushed the backs of his fingers against Tristan's cheek. "Look, Tris, if you want something big and elaborate, you just say the word and I'm all in. Anything you want."

Tristan turned back and gazed into Webber's eyes. "I love you. And for the record, the last thing I want is anything elaborate. Small and intimate is perfect."

Webber leaned back in his seat and closed his eyes. "So tell me what you were imagining earlier," he asked.

"The property is so beautiful, and there are so many little secluded spots here and there, but I fell in love with the formal garden the moment I saw it."

"I know what you mean," Webber agreed. "Every last blade of grass, hedge, and flower is manicured to perfection. And it's so private."

"Exactly," Tristan concurred. "But that aisle is so long. I don't know about you, but I don't like being the center of attention, and if we walked down that long aisle hand in hand, that's precisely what we'll be."

"I see your point," Webber interjected. "So what do we do?"

Tristan rubbed his chin and Webber saw the wheels turning. "What if we have specialty cocktails around the pool with a jazz quartet as people are arriving, and when it's time for the ceremony, we have the jazz quartet lead us along with our guests to the garden and down the aisle sort of like the old jazz bands of New Orleans? When we get to the end of the aisle, the band sets up in the corner of the garden, our guests take their seats, and we stand inside the pergola with the officiant."

Webber felt the grin spread across his face. "I love that idea, Tris. You're a genius."

Tristan continued, his mind obviously still at work, "Then when the ceremony is over, we can have more cocktails and passed hors d'oeuvres while the jazz band plays in the garden and then eventually dinner and dancing."

"Outstanding!" Webber exclaimed. "It sounds just perfect."

Tristan smiled, apparently very pleased with himself. "It is perfect, isn't it?"

"Tomorrow, I'll call Cavan and Sam and see what they think of the idea," Tristan offered. "I'm sure the inn's wedding coordinator can hook us up with all the necessary people."

Webber was warmed to his toes. "I love you; this is going to be so much fun."

"I love you too."

"IT'S good to be home," Tristan said as he slipped his key into the lock and pushed open the massive front door. His sense of smell was immediately assaulted by something really sweet. "Damn, something smells really good," he mumbled almost to himself.

Webber was right behind him, fumbling with both of their overnight bags while trying to close the door. "Sophie! We're home," he yelled, finally kicking the door closed. "Sophie?"

"I'm here, Mr. Kin—I mean, Webber," the housekeeper said as she rounded the corner from the direction of the kitchen. "Sorry," she added. "I guess old habits die hard."

"What smells so good?" Tristan asked as he pecked Sophie on the cheek.

"Welcome home, you two," Sophie said. "And coconut cake, one of Webber's favorites."

Webber smiled broadly. "You're way too good to me," he said, dropping the bags and giving her a hug.

She smacked him on the arm. "Oh stop it, Webber, you know I love doing it."

"Regardless," he said, "I really appreciate it."

"So?" Sophie asked. "I've been on pins and needles. Did everything go okay in Washington?"

"Exceptionally well," Webber said, winking at Tristan. "The SEC has cleared me of any wrongdoing."

"Oh, that's marvelous, Webber," Sophie replied, almost bouncing. "I'm so happy for both of you."

"Well, I'm not out of the woods yet," Webber said. "I still have the—"

Tristan cleared his throat rather loudly and glared at Webber.

"I mean *we* still have the Department of Justice to deal with, but all indications are they will follow the SEC and clear me."

Tristan nodded in victory, tapping Sophie's upper arm with the back of his hand and winking at her. She giggled, blushing just a little before giving them both a hug. "You boys are too cute for words," she said. "Oh, and I figured you'd be tired after traveling and wouldn't want to go out, so I'm making dinner." She turned and headed back to the kitchen. "Is seven okay?" she asked over her shoulder.

Tristan and Webber looked at one another and nodded. "Perfect, thank you, Sophie."

"Now you boys unpack and get some rest before dinner," she said, rounding the corner, her voice drifting away.

Webber looked at Tristan. "You heard the lady."

Tristan chuckled, picking up their bags and heading for their bedroom.

"Hey Tris," Webber called from behind him.

"Yeah?"

"I've been thinking," Webber offered. "Don't you think it's time we get a realtor and start looking for a new house?"

"We already have a house," Tristan yelled back at him.

When Webber reached the bedroom, Tristan was unzipping their bags and starting to remove their dirty clothes. Webber walked up behind him and turned Tristan around so they were face-to-face. "You promised me we would look at new houses together and if we didn't find anything we liked, then and then only would we stay here, remember?"

Tristan rested his hands on Webber's hips. "Come on, you love it here and I love it here, why do we have to move?"

"I'm not saying we *have* to move," Webber insisted. "But maybe we should look. Maybe we'll find something out there that we like better."

Tristan sighed. "If you're really unhappy here, I'll do whatever you want. But please don't do this for me because I'm really starting to feel at home here."

Webber draped his arms over Tristan's shoulders and kissed his lips gently. "I want you to be happy."

"I am happy," Tristan proclaimed. "In fact, the happiest I've ever been in my life. Come on, Webber, what's not to like about living here? This house has everything."

Webber's eyes appeared to be getting teary. "If you're truly happy here," he said, "I won't push it."

"I am," Tristan whispered. "I love you and I love this house."

Webber smiled genuinely. "That brings us to my next question."

Tristan tilted his head to one side, waiting for the topic. "What did you decide to do with your condo?"

"Funny you should bring that up." Tristan hesitated. "I haven't made up my mind because I wanted to talk to you about it, but I think I want to put it on the market."

"Good answer," Webber exclaimed. "That means you trust me and believe in us, and that makes me happier than anything."

Webber again covered Tristan's lips with his own as he pushed Tristan back onto the bed.

"I think the unpacking can wait," Tristan said against Webber's lips as he pushed the suitcases off of the bed, causing quite a thud when they hit the floor.

"I'll say," Webber mumbled as he deepened the kiss.

LONG after dinner and Sophie's coconut cake, Tristan and Webber were snuggled against one another watching the nightly news, half watching and half dozing. Tristan's eyes popped open when he heard Webber's name mentioned on the television. He sat up straight, searching for the remote and trying to raise the volume.

Webber popped up as well, following Tristan's abrupt movement. "Wha... what's wrong, Tris?"

"You're on television." Tristan located the remote and raised the volume. "To repeat our top story, millionaire playboy, businessman, and well-known philanthropist Webber Kincaid has resigned from his position as chairman of the board, president, and CEO of Kincaid International Corporation (KIC). Our sources tell us Mr. Kincaid, along with his chief financial officer, Nathan Bridges, is under investigation by the Securities and Exchange Commission as well as the Department of Justice for unethical behavior for an unknown business acquisition that took place some years back. The SEC and Department of Justice confirmed the investigation, but declined to comment, as did KIC. But in a bizarre and shocking twist to this story, it appears that Kincaid is no longer involved with Deanna Lynn, his longtime girlfriend and well-known supermodel, shown here with Kincaid on the red carpet at last year's Academy Awards."

A picture of Deanna and Webber smiling and posing for the cameras popped up on the screen. "Wow, you look hot," Tristan said with a nervous chuckle, attempting to use humor to lighten the shock and panic he was experiencing.

Webber smacked Tristan on the arm. "Not funny! Hell, they called me a playboy."

The blonde female news anchor with the bright pearly white teeth continued. "Rumored to also be pregnant with Kincaid's baby, Lynn was not available for comment. But sources close to Lynn confirmed the pregnancy and breakup and say that she is totally devastated. The same source also told us Kincaid is now engaged to his former chief administrative assistant, Tristan Paul Moreau, shown here together in the Caribbean a few weeks ago looking quite in love, and walking hand in hand on Martha's Vineyard earlier today."

"Oh my God," Tristan yelled as a shot of him and Webber toasting one another on the bow of the boat in that secluded cove they loved so much flashed across the screen. But before he could say anything else, another picture of them on the Vineyard popped up. "Damn! It's us walking through Edgartown. How can they do this shit so quickly?"

The news anchor continued. "Neither Kincaid nor Moreau could be reached for comment."

Her male co-anchor shook his head. "Man, I didn't see that one coming. But hey, to each his own." He shrugged in a nonchalant manner. "Now let's toss it over to John for a check of tomorrow's weather."

Tristan, still holding the remote, clicked the television off, ran his fingers through his hair, and looked over at Webber, who was staring at the blank television, apparently in shock. "Web?" Tristan whispered. "I'm so sorry."

Webber seemed to snap out of his trance. "Holy shit! Wait, what? What are you sorry for?" he asked, taking Tristan's hand and squeezing. "You didn't do this. I'm the one who should be apologizing to you."

Webber gave Tristan's hand one last squeeze and then released it as he stood and started pacing. Tristan watched Webber closely as he moved back and forth, one hand on his hip and the other rubbing the back of his neck. "Who in the fuck leaked this story? The board agreed that we would do a press conference when the time was right."

Tristan didn't quite know what to say, so he stood up and blocked Webber's pacing. "Stop pacing, you're making me dizzy." He wrapped his arms around him and held him tightly. "We'll figure it out, Web."

"Deanna," he said quietly. "We need to warn Deanna. She's three hours behind us." Before Webber could say another word, Tristan was searching his contacts for Deanna's number. When he heard the call go through, he handed the phone to Webber. Webber continued to pace, holding the phone up to his ear. "No D, it's Webber," he said.

Tristan listened as Webber explained the situation to her. When he was finished filling her in, Webber paused.

"I know, D, but I worry about you—"

"Yeah, he's okay. A little shocked, but okay—" he said, looking over at Tristan

"Hold on."

Webber passed the phone to Tristan. "She wants to talk to you."

Tristan took the phone and put it to his ear, his hand trembling just a little. "Hey, Deanna," he said cautiously.

"Hey, baby," she said with concern in her voice. "How are you holding up, kid?"

"I'm okay," Tristan said hesitantly. "I'm more concerned about you and Webber."

"Honey, we'll be fine. We've both dealt with the press a million times," she insisted. "This will pass with the next big news story."

"I know you guys have dealt with the press," he said, glancing at Webber who was still pacing. Tristan turned his back, put his hand in front of his mouth, and almost whispered the next words. "But Webber's never been outed on the same day his resignation was announced, not to mention the SEC investigation. It's a hell of a lot to handle. Not to mention the fact that they're making it sound like Nathan and Webber were in this together."

"Listen, honey," Deanna insisted. "The truth will come out. Webber's a big boy and trust me, when the shock wears off, he'll move into action. Give him a few minutes and he'll get his butt in gear and kick some paparazzi ass. It's just the way he operates. Hell, I wouldn't be surprised if he wasn't already coming up with a plan."

Tristan knew what Deanna was saying was right. He turned around again and Webber was still pacing, but he could already see his wheels turning. "Thanks, Deanna."

"Tristan, you were outed today too," she said with compassion in her voice. "Are you okay with that?"

"Oh please," Tristan said. "You know how much I love Webber, and I don't care who knows it. I could give a rat's ass about being outed. He's the one I'm worried about."

"Okay, okay. But you call if you need me, alright? My publicist will handle this on my end, so you two just worry about yourselves. This will pass, honey, I promise."

"I know. Bye, Deanna, and thanks."

"Any time, honey. You take care."

Tristan's heartbeat started to return to normal as he handed the phone back to Webber.

He watched closely as Webber listened to whatever Deanna was saying to him, nodding while still rubbing the back of his neck.

"I know, I know, D. Okay. I love you too. Bye."

Webber pressed "End" on Tristan's phone and handed it back to him. "You okay?" he asked again.

"I'm fine. But more importantly, are you okay?"

"I will be," Webber replied hesitantly. "But first I'm gonna call an emergency board meeting for eight o'clock tomorrow morning. Right after the board meeting, we'll meet with the public relations department to prepare a statement and schedule a press conference."

"Thanks for including me in the plan," Tristan said brushing the backs of his fingers against Webber's face.

Webber caught his hand and kissed it. "This involves both of us, baby, and we're in it for better or for worse, remember?" Webber asked. "Your life will be affected by this as much as mine."

Tristan didn't expect the warmth that spread through him with those few simple words, but he found himself barely able to keep the tears at bay. He cleared his throat before trying to speak. "O-okay. So how about if I call half the board members, and you call the other half?"

"Good idea," Webber said, sighing. "I'll take Hillary, Betty, and Bob and you take Scott, John, and Cynthia."

Tristan picked up his phone and started searching his contacts. "I'm on it."

When they were through calling the board members, they compared notes. From the board members Webber had called, Bob was the only one who'd seen the news broadcast, and he was none too happy about it. Out of Tristan's calls, John and Scott had both seen the broadcast and said they'd been expecting the call, and that Webber and Tristan could count on their support.

"So," Webber started. "Don't you think you should call someone in your family and give them the heads up—at least Gage?"

Tristan gave the question some thought. "Not that they care, but maybe they won't see it."

"I'm sorry, baby, but by tomorrow this is going to be on every entertainment news show, not to mention financial news outlets. I feel certain they'll see it."

Tristan sighed. "I'll give Gage a call. He deserves to know."

"Speaking of Gage," Webber asked. "When do I get to meet him? I'd really like to get to know him."

"I'm hoping he and Andy will come to the wedding, but when I talk to him, I'll ask if they can get away before that. Maybe come here, or if things settle down, we can make a short trip to Nashville."

"Either way will be fine with me," Webber offered. "But I'm serious about getting to know them. They're your family, which means in a couple of months they'll be my family too."

Tristan placed a warm kiss on Webber's lips. "Thanks, that means a lot. Here you are worrying about me and my family when your world going to hell in a handbasket."

"My world is just fine as long as you're in it," Webber professed, framing Tristan's face with his hands. "So don't you go worrying about me. We'll deal with this issue just like we're going to deal with anything that comes up in our lives. Besides, we'll be old news in a few days."

"Oh great," Tristan teased. "Now you're telling me my first exposé will be over before it begins."

"I'm afraid so," Webber said, getting to his feet and pulling Tristan up with him. "We've got a very early wakeup call. Why don't we turn in?"

"You go ahead. I'm gonna try and call Gage."

Webber squeezed both Tristan's hands and covered Tristan's lips with his own. "Please give him my best and tell him I'm looking forward to meeting them both."

TRISTAN sat back down on the couch, stretched out, and crossed his legs at the ankles. He dialed his little brother's number, half needing to talk to him and half hoping to get voice mail.

His brother answered with a chuckle. "So, according to the national news, you've been a very busy man lately."

Tristan laughed nervously. "I guess you saw."

"Oh yeah, we saw. First you're engaged to a man being investigated by the SEC, then you're traipsing all over the Caribbean and Martha's Vineyard looking all lovey-dovey and your baby brother knows nothing about any of it? What gives, big bro?"

"I'm sorry, Gage. I know I should have called you guys, but everything just happened so damn fast," Tristan said, leaning forward and rubbing his hand through his hair.

Gage roared with laughter. And to make matters worse, Tristan could hear Andy laughing in the background as well. *Oh great, now they're both laughing at me.*

"Really, Gage?" Tristan huffed. "You're both laughing at me?"

"I'm sorry, Tristan, I know I shouldn't be laughing, but you've got to admit, it's pretty damn funny to this cowboy," Gage admitted.

"Oh please," Tristan said. "Since when did you become a cowboy?"

"Since I moved to Nashville with my boyfriend the cowboy singer," he replied. "Hey, don't make this about me. I'm sure you didn't call to talk about my cowboy status."

"I'm really sorry I haven't called sooner," Tristan confessed. "We've just been caught up in this whirlwind with one thing after another."

He filled Gage in on him and Webber and everything that'd happened in the Caribbean, the SEC and Justice Department investigations, their engagement, and their upcoming marriage on Martha's Vineyard.

"I'd really like to see you guys," Tristan begged. "And I know Webber wants to get to know you. Can you guys make it over to Atlanta anytime soon?"

"I'll talk to Andy and get back to you, but I don't see why not. He doesn't go back out on tour for three more months."

"Is he still touring with Billy Eagan as a backup singer?"

"Yep, but he's doing a few solo gigs here and there in Nashville at Jean's Magnolia Saloon, and he's starting to get a decent following."

"Good for him," Tristan said with pride in his voice. "Every time I hear a Billy Eagan song on the radio, I think of you guys. I love you, little brother."

"I love you too, Tristan. I'll see what we can do to make it over to Atlanta soon."

"And I'll do a better job of keeping you in the loop, I promise. Give my love to Andy."

"Will do, and tell Webber we're looking forward to welcoming him into our very little family. Bye, Tristan."

Tristan thought he heard a crack in Gage's voice, but he had quite a lump in his throat as well, so he wasn't going to bust Gage's chops about it. He'd save that round of teasing for the next time he saw him.

WEBBER woke in a deep fog. He threw his hand back and swiped at the alarm clock several times in an attempt to make the extremely annoying sound go away. When he finally managed to hit the right spot, the alarm silenced, and he rolled over to his back and sighed. Tristan stirred next to him and snuggled in closer, throwing his leg and arm on top of Webber.

"Hell of a night," Tristan admitted with a deep morning voice.

Webber brushed the hair out of Tristan's face. "You could say that. Did you get any sleep at all?" he asked.

"A little, you?"

"A little."

The house phone as well as their cells had started ringing around midnight with everyone and their brother trying to get a statement. Eventually they turned both cell phones off and unplugged the house phone, but by then they were too wired up to sleep.

"The last time I looked at the clock it was four fifteen," Webber admitted. "But I must have dozed off shortly after that because I was out like a light when the alarm went off."

"What time is it?" Tristan asked through a stifled yawn.

Webber turned his head and glanced at the clock. "A little before six," he said, catching the aroma of freshly brewed coffee in the air.

"I love you," Webber said, realizing Tristan must have programmed the coffee maker before he'd come to bed last night.

"Just for my coffee making capabilities," Tristan teased.

"Among others," Webber responded. "You stay put and I'll get us a cup so when we turn on the television, we'll have something to ease the blow."

Tristan didn't argue. Instead, the minute Webber rolled out of bed, he rolled into his spot and curled into a ball, pulling the covers over his head. Webber chuckled and rubbed Tristan's head through the covers.

"I'll be right back, sleepyhead."

Webber watched as Tristan briefly stuck his head out from under the covers. "Hurry!" he demanded, burrowing back into his warm cocoon again.

"Yes sir," Webber promised.

Five minutes later Webber was back with two steaming cups of coffee. He placed one on Tristan's bedside table. "You ready to see what the news is saying about us this morning?" he asked, picking up the remote and waving it around.

Webber smiled as Tristan slid back over to his side of the bed, sat up straight, smoothed his hair, and raised the blanket, inviting Webber to come back and join him. "How do I look?" he asked with a lopsided grin.

"As gorgeous as ever," Webber replied.

"Then I guess I'm ready," Tristan said, still holding up the blankets.

Webber slipped back in bed, trying not to spill his coffee, still clutching the remote control in his other hand. Once he was nestled at Tristan's side, he turned on the television.

George Stephanopoulos of *Good Morning America* was reviewing the top new stories of the morning, and Webber nervously waited for the bomb to drop, but George finished without one mention of their names. "Wow," Webber said. "Nothing."

The camera then panned over to Lara Spencer as she began the "Pop News" segment. "We've been following a story that broke last night regarding millionaire Webber Kincaid, chairman, president, and CEO of Kincaid International," she reported. "Apparently Kincaid resigned after allegations that he and his former CFO Nathan Bridges were caught overinflating the price of a past acquisition by the SEC and Department of Justice and pocketing the difference."

Lara smiled into the camera as she continued. "But the intriguing part of this story has to do with Kincaid's personal life. According to our sources, he's apparently left his longtime girlfriend Deanna Lynn, who is rumored to be carrying his baby, for his former personal assistant." There was a gasp from Sam Champion and Robin Roberts. "But that's not the best part," Lara continued. "Wait for it, wait for it. His former assistant is a man named Tristan Paul Moreau."

"Jesus Christ!" Webber said as more pictures of him and Tristan flashed across the screen. There were pictures of him and Tristan in the Caribbean sitting on the dock, them lounging on the terrace around the pool, one of the same shots from last night with them on the bow of the boat, and even pictures of them riding the golf cart around the island.

"It appears that Kincaid and Moreau have been quite cozy for some time, as seen by these photos taken in the Caribbean a few weeks ago and more recently on Martha's Vineyard where they were supposedly looking for a wedding venue."

There were more pictures of Tristan and Webber getting off the plane at Martha's Vineyard Airport, holding hands on the streets of Edgartown, and checking out the cliffs in Aquinnah.

"Where do they get this information?" Tristan asked, looking concerned.

"Anywhere and everywhere they can," Webber explained.

"Neither of the men returned our calls for comment."

"In a statement from Deanna Lynn's publicist, she confirmed that she is indeed pregnant, but it is not Kincaid's baby, and says they've never been more than best friends and she is thrilled for him and Moreau. Which begs the question," Lara continued. "If it's not Kincaid's baby, then whose is it? Another story for another day," she added.

Tristan and Webber looked at each other and smiled. "Thata girl, Deanna," Webber said.

"She's the best," Tristan agreed.

Webber turned the channel to NBC, where Matt Lauer of the *Today* show was in the middle of his commentary. He covered everything *Good Morning America* did, but went so far as to say that the SEC had suspended their investigation of Kincaid, but that an indictment of his former CFO was imminent.

"Well, have you seen enough?" Webber asked, aiming the remote control at the television but not pressing the off button.

"Enough for a lifetime," Tristan whispered. He quietly took the last sip of his coffee and put the empty cup on his bedside table. He pulled back the covers and attempted to get out of bed.

Webber placed his hand on Tristan's shoulder. "Baby, talk to me," he whispered, kissing Tristan on his bare shoulder.

Tristan froze. "It's not you, Web. I just don't want to be known as a home wrecker, that's all."

"I know, baby," Webber assured him. "No more than I want to be found guilty in the court of personal opinion for the things I'm being accused of, especially when it involves Nathan Bridges."

Tristan took a deep breath. "You're right. I'm being selfish. I'm sorry."

"No, Tristan. You're not being selfish. Who wants to deal with this crap? It's not fair to either of us, but we'll get through it."

"You know what really bothers me?" Tristan admitted. "I really couldn't care less about what my parents and older brother think of me, but I sure as hell hate to give them more shit to use against me."

Webber looked down into his empty coffee cup, not sure what to say. "I hate that, too, and I'm sorry," was all he could think of. "I promise we'll clear up all these misconceptions at our press conference and set the record straight," he stated. "In fact, I think I'm gonna ask Deanna to be here in person to give her statement. I think the show of unity will go a long way."

"I agree, but isn't the damage already done?" Tristan asked. "I mean, the accusations are already out there. Do you really think the majority of the people out there care if they're true or not?"

"Sadly, no," Webber admitted. "And you're right about the information already being out there, but think about it, Tristan. With today's social media, people can say anything they want about you, true or false, and you can't do a damn thing about it."

Tristan sighed and turned to face Webber. "You're right. I know you are," he said, taking Webber's hand. "I guess I just need to grow a thicker skin."

Tristan was looking down at their joined hands. Webber placed his forefinger under Tristan's chin and raised his head until their eyes met. "There's the Tristan Moreau I know and love with all my heart." His lips covered Tristan's in a sweet, gentle kiss.

"How do you do it, Web?" Tristan asked when the kiss ended.

"Well, for starters, I just tell myself that the people we care about and those who care about us will know the truth, and that's all that matters."

"You make it sound so easy," Tristan murmured.

"It's as easy as we make it," Webber stated. "Look, I love you with all my heart, and I'm past worrying about what other people think of me. I no longer have KIC to worry about, and I have everything I want right here in front of me. And besides, all of this will blow over as soon as Lindsay Lohan runs down her next victim, and with her record, that could be as early as this afternoon."

At first Tristan smiled a little at the comment. Then Webber watched as the small smile spread across his face until he was beaming. "You're right," he said in a teasing tone. "The odds are, if she doesn't run someone down or claim she's been assaulted, she'll at least have another fender bender, right?"

"Absolutely," Webber said with a roar of laughter.

Tristan threw himself on top of Webber, tackling him in the middle of the bed. When he had Webber pinned down under him, he put his face close to Webber's ear. "You're lucky we have to get to the office or I'd punish you for all this drama right here and now," he said breathlessly.

Webber felt chills race up and down his spine at the sheer tone of Tristan's voice. "Oh please, promise me that you'll punish me tonight, then," he begged.

"Maybe, maybe not," Tristan teased, stealing a kiss and then hopping out of bed and heading for the bathroom.

"Wait for me," Webber yelled. "You're not getting in that big shower all by yourself."

WEBBER was the last one to enter the boardroom, leaving Tristan nervously pacing outside. He wanted Tristan with him, but he also knew it would have been inappropriate to ask the board to allow him to attend the meeting since he was not a formal member of the board of directors nor was he a KIC employee any longer. Additionally, Webber knew he was personally going to be under fire for all of this, although he did nothing wrong and had no control over what got leaked to the press, and he was grateful Tristan would not be subjected to the same ridicule. He would take the abuse from the board for the sake of the company, but his main objective was to do whatever he had to do to get the board to prepare a statement for the press showing support and clearing him from any wrongdoing. He also had to convince the board to allow him to make certain statements about his personal life within the confines of the corporate press conference, and he could do that by making them see that these type of questions were going to come up, so he may as well address them in the press conference rather than allowing them to surface during Q&A.

The members of the board were all seated at the conference table with eyes on Webber as he stood at the head of the table. Webber cleared his throat before he spoke. "Members of the board, you'll have to excuse me as I don't know the protocol for leading the board meeting since you have already accepted my resignation but haven't found my replacement. Would one of you like to do the honors?"

The board members exchanged glances, but no one volunteered. Hillary Jordan was the first to speak. "Webber, I think I speak for the entire board," she said, looking around at her fellow board members, "when I ask that you chair the meeting as usual. You've been at the helm of KIC since your father's passing and have done a spectacular job of building this company to what it is today. We as a board forget to mention that sometimes. So please do the honors."

Webber mouthed "thank you" to Hillary and smiled humbly as he nodded to the rest of the board and called the meeting to order. "Since you asked me to chair the meeting, I would like to say a few words before we get started," Webber stated.

The board again looked around the room, most nodding in approval, a couple looking stoic but not happy.

"Members of the board," he said looking around the room, palms flat on the table. "I've spent all of my adult life running this company. I've done it respectfully with as much dignity as I could, and I will hold my head high when I walk out of here for the last time. But let me make one thing very clear. As long as I'm here, and as long as I'm a major stockholder in the company, I will not tolerate any disrespect regarding my personal life. I've lived my life scandal-free by hiding behind a dear friend and, even worse than that, hiding from myself."

Webber removed his palms from the surface of the table and rubbed his hands together as he took a step back. "I'm sure you all saw the photos of Tristan and me, both in the Caribbean and on Martha's Vineyard, and I will not, let me repeat, I will not apologize for living my life. Some, hell, maybe even all of you may not understand my lifestyle, but it is just that, my lifestyle. It's not for you to approve or disapprove," Webber said, looking mostly at Robert Yellos. "Today I want to prepare a statement regarding the investigation, my resignation, and, of course, address questions about Tristan, Deanna, and me. Questions about my personal life are bound to come up in Q&A, and rather than dodge them, I'd like to hit them head-on. I would like to do all of this at a press conference tomorrow afternoon."

Webber scanned the room and no one was showing any signs of stopping him, so he went on. "If I have your complete support, I will work right along with you as long as it takes to get a statement we are all happy with. But if you feel you cannot support me, I will leave you alone to determine the type of statement you want to make and allow you to make it with no interference. In return, Tristan, Deanna, and I will hold our own press conference, in which you will have no input, and explain the investigation, my resignation, and clear up all the speculation regarding our personal lives."

Webber sighed and took a seat. "I'd be more than happy to step out if you would like to put the options to a vote."

John Reynolds stood up. "I would like to propose that the board work along with Webber to produce a favorable outcome for KIC as well as him and Tristan."

"I second," Hillary said.

John spoke again. "All in favor, please say 'aye'."

The room was filled with a chorus of ayes.

"All not in favor say 'nay'."

There was one lone nay, and Webber knew from whom it came without even looking up. Robert Yellos stood and slammed his fist into the table, causing everyone to jump in surprise. His face was beet red and contorted into a painful expression. "I can't believe all of you would support this type of behavior. Cavorting around God knows where, putting yourself in a position to have questionable pictures taken of you in compromising situations is unacceptable behavior for anyone, not to mention a man in your position. I can't believe that all of you are turning a blind eye to this mockery of leadership."

Robert took a deep breath, smoothed the front of his business suit, and spoke in a calmer tone. "Unfortunately, I cannot condone this behavior, nor can I watch you take KIC down with you."

Robert turned his hateful gaze to Webber. "Your father would be as appalled as I am at your recent behavior, or, what do you call it, your coming out of the closet." He then looked around the room and continued. "It appears to me that all of you have made your decision to stand behind this abomination and if that is indeed the case, I must resign my seat on this board effective immediately. Good day!" Robert huffed as he grabbed his briefcase from the chair next to him and headed for the boardroom door. When he opened the door, Webber saw Tristan still pacing where he'd left him and got up from his seat to head off any confrontation. Robert opened his mouth, apparently to speak to Tristan, but before he could say a word, Webber yelled, "Not a word, Robert. Leave him alone. Your fight is not with him; it's with me."

Robert stopped and looked at Webber with disdain. "Neither of you are worth it." He turned and stormed off toward the elevator.

Tristan had a look of shock and confusion on his face. Webber walked over to close the door again and stopped. "I'll explain later," he whispered.

"Would Tristan like to join the meeting?" Scott Mullin asked. "I know it's not normal protocol, but the only business on the agenda for today's meeting deeply involves him and I think it's only fair that he's part of the discussion," Scott continued. "Does anyone have any issues with that?"

Webber was shocked, as was Tristan, who had overheard the invitation. No one objected, and Webber held out his hand to Tristan and welcomed him into the meeting.

Webber was choking up from the level of support his board was showing him, and suddenly he was struggling to hold back the tears. "Thank you all for allowing Tristan to join us," he said, his voice cracking once or twice. "I'll never forget what happened here today, and I will be forever grateful for your unwavering support."

Tristan thanked everyone as well and quietly took a seat.

From that point, the meeting was very productive, with no signs of tension or discomfort in the room. Everyone worked together like a well-oiled machine, and by midday, the statement, which covered the SEC investigation, Webber's resignation, the charges against Nathan Bridges, and Webber and Tristan's personal admissions, was drafted and approved.

In addition, in a strong show of support, the board members agreed to attend the press conference and be available to answer any questions should they be needed. Webber had placed a call to Deanna and she agreed to attend as well. Tristan slipped out of the meeting long enough to schedule a jet to pick her up, which was already in the air, so everything was coming together nicely.

When the board meeting finally ended and heartfelt thanks and good-byes were exchanged, Webber and Tristan met with KIC's public relations department. By late afternoon, the press release was written, approved, and scheduled to hit the newswire just after the close of the stock market. The press conference was scheduled for two o'clock the next day at the Ritz Carlton Buckhead, and Webber instructed his PR team to contact all media outlets and alert them to the conference prior to the release to help beef up attendance. In addition, he'd added all the entertainment news outlets to the list of business and financial contacts in hopes that they could get this done in one fell swoop.

"Well," Webber said, looking at Tristan sitting across his desk and stuffing a copy of the press release into his Coach bag. "I think we've crossed all the t's and dotted all the i's. What do you say we call it a day?"

"Yes, sir," Tristan said, adding a mock salute. "I'm worn out too."

Webber leaned back in his chair and linked his fingers across his stomach. "It's been a long one, all right, but very enlightening and highly productive, wouldn't you say?"

"I guess you could say that," Tristan said, shaking his head and chuckling. "I still can't believe Mr. Yellos resigned and stormed out of the meeting."

"Good riddance," Webber said with a wave of his hand. "But putting all the drama aside, it was nice working side by side with you again, almost like old times."

"Except now I get to go home *with* you instead of going home alone and pining for you," Tristan teased, giving Webber a wink. "But it was fun working together today."

"Do you miss it, Tris?" Webber asked sincerely.

Tristan thought about the question for a minute. "Not really," he replied with a tilt of his head. "The best part of my job was spending time with you. And since I get to do it all the time now, I don't think I'm gonna miss the job one bit." Tristan held up a hand. "I mean… don't get me wrong. Sometimes I loved getting lost in my job, but I think that was a way of dealing with my frustration in regards to the way I felt about you."

Webber raised an eyebrow. "Felt?" he asked.

"Yeah. I'm over it now that I actually have you," Tristan said in a serious tone. "The anticipation was way better than the real thing."

Before Webber could respond, Tristan burst into laughter. "I thought I could say that with a straight face, but I guess the laugh's on me."

Webber had to admit the words did send a little pang of sadness to his heart, although he felt certain Tristan was teasing him. He couldn't imagine what he would do if Tristan ever said those words and meant them. He shook the thought out of his head and smiled. "I think we need to get home. I seem to remember something about a punishment."

Tristan wiggled his eyebrows in a sinister way and stood. "By all means then. Let the punishment begin."

WHEN they walked through their front door, Deanna was sprawled out on the couch wearing turquoise slacks and a glittery turquoise and blue chiffon top. What was left of the setting sun was peeking through the french doors and reflecting off of her blonde locks. Her spike-heel-clad feet were propped up on the arm of the couch, and she was flipping through a magazine. By the looks of it, she must have just finished a snack and a cup of tea Sophie had obviously prepared for her. Webber thought he had never seen her look more beautiful.

"It's about time," she said without looking up from her magazine.

"That's a fine welcome," Webber said. "Aren't you going to get up?"

She burst into laughter. "Oh, honey, I would if I could," she said, motioning for one of them to come and help her. Tristan made it to the couch before Webber and offered his hand, lifting her to her feet. She threw her arms around his neck and kissed his cheek. She stepped back to take both of his hands in hers and looked him in the eye. "How're you doing, honey?"

"I'm good," he replied.

"Really?" she asked.

Tristan thought about it for a second. "Yeah, I am. Webber and I spent all day getting the press release ready, and the press conference is tomorrow afternoon, so hopefully by the end of the day tomorrow, this will all be behind us."

"Pretty good attitude for a home wrecker," she said with a wink, releasing his hands and turning her attention to Webber. "And you, my supposed baby daddy?" she said in a singsong voice. "Are you okay?"

Webber chuckled as he took in his best friend's appearance. "I'm good, but you look like you swallowed a basketball."

"Oh, Tristan," she said, looking away from Webber. "How do you put up with this man?" She turned back to Webber. "I know, isn't it awful. I *feel* like I swallowed a basketball."

Webber put his Coach bag down on the chair and walked over to her. "Seriously, D, I don't think I've ever seen you looking more beautiful."

"Really," she said, smoothing the front of her outfit and rubbing her baby bump. "I don't feel very attractive."

"He's right," Tristan said. "You're absolutely radiant."

"Oh hell," she giggled. "Who can argue with you two; I am radiant, aren't I?"

Webber pulled her into his arms and hugged her tightly. "You are," he whispered, winking at Tristan over her shoulder.

"Oh, enough about me," Deanna said. "Tell me about the press conference."

"In a little while," Webber said. "Give Tristan and me a couple of minutes to get changed. And what's the chance that while we're changing, you can be a dutiful baby mama and fix us a scotch?"

"I'll see if I can arrange that," she replied. "But you two better hurry, and no hanky-panky in there until bedtime. Got it?"

"You're very bossy," Webber teased, taking Tristan by the hand and dragging him in the direction of the bedroom.

"Just remember what I said," Deanna yelled over her shoulder while rummaging through the bar for the single malt. "Don't make me come in there and get you."

"Yes, ma'am," Tristan managed to get out right before Webber closed the bedroom door.

Ten minutes later they were changed and about to join Deanna again, Webber barefoot in blue jeans and a black Henley and Tristan in blue jeans and a button down. Webber was waiting for Tristan to come out of the bedroom when he heard Deanna at the piano. He stopped and listened, knowing she was a trained pianist, but never remembering how beautifully she played. When Tristan joined him, they walked hand in hand through the foyer and stopped just before she could see them and watched. She was poised at the large grand piano, looking as stunning as ever. "She's amazing," Tristan whispered just loud enough for Webber to hear.

"I forget sometimes just how amazing," Webber admitted. "She's hot, smart, and has such a great heart; I almost wished she was carrying our baby. That baby can't lose with a mother like her."

Tristan didn't respond right away. They'd never discussed having children. Had Tristan assumed Webber didn't want any?

"Would you like to be a father one day?" Tristan asked, quietly enough that Deanna couldn't hear him.

"Oh, I don't know," Webber shared. "I never thought about it much before now, but she looks so happy. What about you, do you want kids?"

"I don't know either," Tristan replied. "I mean... I think I would be a good father, but my life was never really conducive to having a baby, so I never gave it any real thought."

"Well, maybe we should," Webber concluded. "Give it some real thought, I mean."

Tristan nodded. "I love you."

"I love you too."

Suddenly the music stopped. "What are you two whispering about over there?" Deanna asked.

Webber laughed out loud. "And she has great hearing," he whispered.

"I heard that," she said, getting up from the piano.

They walked across the foyer and stopped. "We were just listening to how beautifully you play," Tristan said genuinely.

"I'm so rusty," Deanna whined. "But I read somewhere that it's good for the baby, so I recently started playing again."

"Good for you!" Webber said, clearing his throat. "Now where are our drinks, woman?"

Deanna smirked and pointed to the bar. "As requested, your majesty."

"Fine then," Webber mocked. "You get to keep your head for another day."

"Oh thanks a lot," Deanna murmured.

Webber walked over and picked up the two glasses and handed one to Tristan. "Why don't we take these to the den," he suggested. "On the way, we can stop in the kitchen, say hi to Sophie, and see what she's working on for dinner."

"Okay by me," Tristan answered, looking at Deanna.

"Me too," she said, linking her arms in theirs. "Lead the way, gentlemen."

After checking in with Sophie, who confirmed they had about an hour before dinner, they all got comfortable in the den, Webber and Tristan side by side on one couch and Deanna stretched out on the other. Webber filled her in on everything they'd put in the press release and all that had happened during the very long day. Deanna explained that she and her publicist had agreed that she would make it perfectly clear she and Webber were never more than best friends, Tristan was not a home wrecker, and Webber was not the father of her child. But they decided to stop short of revealing the true father's identity, leaving it open to speculation. She also asked to have a copy of the press release sent to her publicist so everyone would be on the same page when the calls started to come in.

"Now that the business stuff is all out of the way, tell me about Martha's Vineyard. Don't you just love it?"

Webber glanced at Tristan. "We do. In fact, it's the perfect place to get married. It's private and secluded and has everything we want. Even Cavan and Sam, the owners, are great."

Deanna clapped her hands together quickly. "I'm so excited. When is this soirée going to take place?"

"September fifteenth at three o'clock in the afternoon," Tristan said proudly.

"No! Not this September?" Deanna moaned.

"Yes. This September. Why?" Webber asked.

"Oh God," she surmised. "I'm gonna look like the Goodyear blimp by then."

Webber threw his head back in laughter. "So now you're expecting us to postpone our wedding until you're a size two again?"

Deanna frowned. "I guess not. That would be pretty selfish."

"I'm glad you recognized that so quickly," Webber teased.

Deanna took one of her shoes off and threw it at Webber, the tip of the spike heel almost catching him in the cheek. "You're a very funny man, Webber Kincaid."

"Hey!" Tristan said. "Don't ruin that handsome face."

"I wouldn't dream of it," Deanna snickered. "But if I'm gonna look like a blimp, you have to promise me that you won't allow anyone to take any pictures of me."

"Isn't that pretty shallow and self-centered on your part?" Webber asked.

"And what's your point?" Deanna shot right back.

"You're right," Webber retorted. "My mistake."

"I thought so," Deanna said, getting up from the couch and hobbling toward the door with one shoe on. "Damn, it feels like I have an anvil sitting on my bladder. Excuse me, boys, I've got to pee."

"Thanks for announcing," Webber responded, holding a pillow in front of his face in case she threw the other shoe. But he was safe; she just glared at him as she hobbled out of the room.

Webber turned, putting his bare feet up on the couch and leaning in against Tristan's chest while draping Tristan's arm around him. "Tristan?"

"Yeah?"

"What do you think about me asking Deanna to be my best gal?"

"I think that's a great idea," Tristan assured him. "You know I adore her."

"Thanks, I just wanted to make sure before I asked. What about you? Do you have anyone in mind?"

"I was hoping Gage would stand up for me," Tristan confessed. "I was planning to ask him if they make it to Atlanta."

Webber held Tristan's arm with both of his hands and pressed it tightly against his chest. "I think that's a perfect idea."

Deanna came back carrying her other shoe in her hand just as Sophie called everyone to dinner. She tossed it to the floor near the other one, then passed them by and headed right for the table.

Webber twisted his head and looked up at Tristan. "I guess she's bellying up to the feeding trough," he whispered.

"I heard that too," Deanna bellowed from the dining room.

"Damn, she's good," Webber joked, getting to his feet and offering his hands to Tristan. "Let's eat."

Sophie served her famous chicken cordon bleu over mashed potatoes and grilled asparagus along with a spinach salad. Everyone agreed the meal was out of this world. After dinner, Sophie shooed them back into the den with a promise to bring fresh coffee and coconut cake shortly. Deanna burrowed back into her couch, coiled up like a rattlesnake, and closed her eyes while Tristan and Webber snuggled back into their spot on the other couch. With everyone comfortable and sated, Webber saw this as the perfect time to pop the question. "Hey D?" he said, twisting his head again and winking at Tristan.

Deanna opened one eye, but didn't say anything. "What do you think about being my best gal at the wedding?"

Both of her eyes sprung open, and she rose up to her elbows with a huge smile on her face. "Are you serious?"

"Of course I'm serious," Webber promised. "You're my best friend."

"Yes! Yes! I'd be honored." Then her expression of joy changed to one of sadness. "But I'm gonna be a blimp and now I'll surely have my picture taken."

Webber smiled, knowing this was difficult for her, but not cutting her any slack. "I guess I can ask someone else if you don't want to do it."

"Webber Kincaid. If you do, I'll never speak to you again."

Webber smiled. "Then it's settled."

Deanna's frown softened a little and eventually morphed into a smile. "I'd love to stand up for the both of you. Hey, I've got an idea. What if we sell ad space on my belly to help pay for the wedding."

Everyone was still roaring with laughter as Sophie came in carrying a large silver tray. After dessert and coffee, they watched the news reports repeating the same old stories and photographs from the night before.

"I think it's time for me to turn in," Deanna said, stifling a yawn.

"Me too," Tristan said as Deanna's yawn triggered his own. "We have a big day tomorrow."

Deanna got to her feet and started loading the silver tray with the dirty dessert dishes. When she was through, Webber carried it to the kitchen and loaded the dishwasher, having long sent Sophie home. Tristan stayed behind and straightened up the den, everyone meeting in the hall on the way to bed.

"See you boys in the morning," Deanna said, scratching her baby bump and kissing them each on the cheek.

"Sleep tight," Tristan said, taking Webber's hand.

As Deanna turned, Webber smacked her on the butt with his free hand. "Goodnight. D, see you in the morning."

She looked over her shoulder, rolled her eyes, and flashed him that million-dollar smile and then blew him a kiss.

THE next morning Webber was the last one to breakfast, but as he approached the dining room, he could hear chattering and laughing, so he stopped and leaned against the doorjamb, savoring the happy sounds. There was no talk of the press conferences or the SEC investigation of late, just friends chatting about what was happening in each other's lives. Webber smiled as he listened to Deanna telling Tristan about the decor she was considering for the baby's room. She rambled on about not wanting to know the baby's sex until he or she was born, which left her unable to do the standard blue or pink, so she decided to have the walls painted a soft mint green. She went on and on about the hand-painted mural covering two of the walls and most of the ceiling. Her smile was beaming as she described in detail the mural featuring a big wispy tree with a hollowed-out trunk and a family of bunny rabbits taking up residence. She giggled as she explained the various redbirds, sparrows, and bluebirds watching over their nests, some full of baby birds with their mouths wide open, while others had mama and papa birds watching over speckled eggs, eagerly waiting for them to hatch. She reached out and touched Tristan's arm when she described the hummingbirds drinking from nectar feeders hanging from the branches, and of course the obvious squirrels and chipmunks running amuck. Then Webber listened as she changed the topic to the full suite of yellow baby furniture she'd ordered, with distressed shades of green peeking through the yellow finish. Webber had never seen her so happy, and it warmed him to his heart. In addition, the fact that she and Tristan seemed to genuinely care for one another was simply icing on the cake. *If we can just get through today, this is what we have to look forward to.*

He cleared his throat and entered the room, both of them turning their heads in his direction. "There you are, sleepyhead," Deanna said. "I've about bored poor Tristan to death with all the details of the baby's room."

"Nonsense," Tristan said with a wave of his hand. "I love hearing all about it."

Webber went to the sideboard, poured himself a cup of coffee, and picked up a cheese danish. On the way to his seat, he put his coffee down on the table and rested his hand on Tristan's shoulder while kissing the top of his head.

Tristan covered Webber's hand with his own and squeezed. "I hope you don't mind that I let you sleep in. You looked so peaceful; I didn't have the heart to wake you."

"Well, I can't say that I didn't enjoy the few extra minutes," Webber insisted. "But I hate that I missed all the girl talk."

Deanna smirked. "Very funny. But if you insist, I can certainly go through all the details again."

"I wouldn't dream of making you do that." Webber chuckled. "Besides, I heard most of it from the doorway."

"Were you eavesdropping, Webber Kincaid?" Deanna teased.

"I guess I was, but it's hardly eavesdropping if it's not a secret."

"Good point," Tristan said, looking at his watch. "I had Sophie make your usual and it should be ready any minute. I was just about to wake you."

Webber reached over and covered Tristan's hand. "Thanks, baby."

Tristan winked. "If you'll excuse me," he said. "I'm gonna jump in the shower and give you two a little private time."

Tristan wiped the corners of his mouth with his napkin and stood just as Sophie popped into the dining room with Webber's vegetable and cheese omelet and bowl of fresh fruit.

"Thanks, Sophie. Perfect as usual," Tristan said.

"Thank you, Tristan, and good morning, Webber," Sophie said, placing the plate in front of him. "I trust you had a good night?"

"I did, Sophie, thank you. How are you this morning?"

"Me? Oh I'm just fine, thank you for asking," Sophie gushed as she cleared Deanna's and Tristan's plates. "Can I get you anything else, Deanna?" she added.

Deanna propped her elbows up on the table and rested her chin in her hands, staring at Webber. "No ma'am, I'm stuffed," she replied. "But thank you for asking." She winked at Sophie. "However, I do think I'm going to sit here and watch Webber eat," she added.

"Oh great," Webber mumbled while chewing on a piece of grapefruit.

"Oh great," Deanna said in a mocking tone, shaking her head. She said nothing else, but simply stared at him.

Webber felt her gaze and eventually looked up from his food. "Whaaat?"

She titled her head to one side. "Honey, I know you're going through some stuff right now, but despite all of it, I've never seen you look happier."

Webber chewed on another bite of omelet and thought about Deanna's statement. After he swallowed, he wiped his mouth with his napkin. "Despite all of it, D, I don't think I've ever been happier," he said, truly meaning it.

"I adore Tristan," she said with a warm smile.

"That makes two of us," Webber replied, smiling right back at her. "I'm one lucky man."

"Oh, don't sell yourself short," she warned. "He's just as lucky."

"Let's just say we're great together and leave it at that," he proclaimed. "And what about you? Any word from Sebastian?"

"Nothing so far."

"That's good," Webber said. "I'm so damned afraid that he's going to have a change of heart and try to take the baby from you."

"I've had that same fear," Deanna said with a concerned tone in her voice. "So I had my attorney draw up a document that in essence takes away all of his rights as a father."

"Has he signed it?"

"Not yet, but according to my attorney, he just got it yesterday."

"I'll keep my fingers crossed," Webber promised. "If you need any help with that, you'll come to me, right?"

"Of course I will. I'll do anything to protect this baby."

Before Webber could respond, Tristan bounced back into the room, looking incredible in a black suit with a silvery grey dress shirt and matching tone-on-tone silk tie. "Wow! You look great."

"Thanks! Am I interrupting anything?"

"No," Deanna said nervously, "but now that you're both here, I'd like to ask you something."

Tristan walked over and stood behind Webber's chair, resting his hands on Webber's shoulders, and waited.

Deanna hesitated for a few seconds, and then spoke. "I'm not quite sure how to say this, so please bear with me."

Webber looked up at Tristan, a bit of concern washing over him. Tristan must have picked up on his concern because he massaged Webber's shoulders in a slow, calming motion. Webber looked back to Deanna.

Deanna cleared her throat before she spoke again. "Okay, so you know I love you guys with all my heart, right?"

Before they could respond, she started anxiously rambling again. "This baby is going to be so lucky to have you in his or her life, and I know you'll love the little bugger as much as I do. And I'm not sure if you know this, Tristan, but my mother is deceased and my father is well on in his years, and since I'm going to be a single mother, I want to make sure my baby is taken care of if something should ever happen to me."

She paused and looked down at her lap as if the words she needed were written on her breakfast napkin. She looked up through her eyelashes hesitantly. "Would you guys be willing to be my baby's godparents?"

Webber felt Tristan squeeze his shoulders as a lump started to form in his throat. His heartbeat raced as tears stung the backs of his eyes.

Deanna's voice interrupted his thoughts. "I know it's a lot to ask, but I wouldn't want anyone else raising my child if anything ever happened to me. If you need time to think it over, please feel free to take as much time as you need."

"No!" Tristan shouted, startling Webber.

Webber could feel Tristan's hands shaking as they rested on his shoulders. He looked up, awkwardly turning in his seat, needing to see Tristan's face. His lover's mouth was hanging open in surprise, but as soon as their eyes met, Webber realized Tristan's expression was of sheer happiness. Staring into those beautiful hazel eyes, shimmering with flecks of green and gold, he was never more in love with Tristan than he was right this very second.

They starred into each other's eyes momentarily and Webber nodded, knowing Tristan understood him.

Deanna's expression turned sad and she sat up straight in her chair. "I know. It's a big responsibility. I'm sorry to have put you on the spot like this."

Tristan looked over at Deanna. "I meant no, we don't need any time to think it over," he blurted out. Webber jumped out of his chair, lifted Tristan off of the ground, and spun him around a few times before righting him back to his feet.

Deanna observed with a stunned look on her face.

"We would be honored," Webber said as he and Tristan ran over to her and threw their arms around her neck.

She struggled to get to her feet, wiping her eyes with the backs of her hands. Webber took her into his arms, his heart so full and his eyes overflowing with tears of joy. He reached for Tristan and the three of them stood embracing one another for the longest time.

When they were able to compose themselves again, Deanna blotted her cheeks with a tissue Webber had given her. "You guys scared me for a second when Tristan yelled 'No'," she said with a weak smile. "I've already changed my will to appoint you as legal guardians should anything happen to me."

"Sorry," Tristan said, sheepishly taking Webber's hand. "We'd be honored."

Five

THE limousine pulled up in front of the Ritz Carlton and Webber was the first to exit. Tristan was next and once out, he turned and offered Deanna his hand as she threw her high-heeled foot out of the car and made contact with the pavement. Together, they walked past the doorman, through the lobby to the meeting room area, and eventually into a suite adjoining the grand ballroom.

Once inside, Webber greeted the PR staff and members of the board who were already accounted for and anxiously approached the door leading to the ballroom. He opened it slightly and stared out into the crowd. The only way he could describe the organized chaos was as a media circus, pure and simple. All the financial news outlets, including Bloomberg, MSNBC, CNN, and CNBC, were there alongside entertainment news networks like E!, BRAVO, and OWN, and that was just the beginning. CBS, ABC, and NBC were represented, as well as many smaller networks, including news magazines like *People*, *The Enquirer*, *Entertainment Weekly*, and *TMZ*. The room was virtually humming from all the energy of the cameras and microphones as everyone seemed to be doing sound checks and testing their broadcast feeds.

The stage directly in front of him was approximately ten feet by thirty feet and roughly three feet off of the ground by his estimation. It held one single podium in front of a cluster of microphones, and beyond that the press was taking up every imaginable square foot of space as far as he could see. He closed the door and turned to find

Tristan looking over his shoulder. Giving Tristan the once-over, Webber thought he seemed a little pale but still looked as gorgeous as ever. He took Tristan's hands and held them tightly. "You ready for this?"

Webber registered Tristan's Adam's apple bobbing with an obvious swallow before he answered. He felt a pang of guilt for putting him through all of this.

"Don't worry about me." Tristan chuckled. "I want to do this so we can put it all behind us and move on with our lives... and I want everyone to know the truth. I'm fine, really."

"Then let's do it," Webber said with a smile and a wink. "I love you."

"I love you too," Tristan whispered.

Just then a PR assistant approached, carrying a wireless microphone. As he was being wired, Webber looked around the room. "Do you see Deanna?"

Tristan did a quick scan and pointed. "There she is."

Webber followed Tristan's gaze and in the corner, seemingly uninterested in all that was going on around her, Deanna was seated comfortably, looking into a compact mirror and applying lipstick.

Webber howled. "Always the supermodel," he teased. When the assistant was through wiring him, he took Tristan by the hand and led him over to Deanna.

She looked up over her compact. "Might I help you?" she asked in a playful tone.

"It's show time, D," Webber said, offering her his hand.

She closed her compact and put it, along with her lipstick, in her handbag and took his hand, flashing him that supermodel smile.

"Ever the calm one," Webber said.

"Oh, honey, this is a cakewalk compared to being backstage for a fashion show with one hundred screaming women," she teased.

The board of directors lined up single file and exited the room, taking the two steps up to the stage and standing to the right of the podium. Next, the head of the PR department walked over to the podium and stood until the room became silent. "Ladies and gentle of the press, I'd like to introduce the Chairman of the Board, President, and Chief Executive Office of Kincaid International Corporation, Mr. Webber Kincaid."

Webber and Tristan entered with Deanna between them, her arms hanging loosely in each of theirs. She appeared strong and confident, looking stunning in an emerald-green silk pantsuit accentuating her baby bump and her golden-blonde hair pulled up into a french twist. Tristan was still in the handsome black suit he had chosen earlier, and Webber had opted for a navy blue suit with an ecru shirt and gold, navy, and red striped tie.

Just before they reached the podium, Deanna released Webber's arm and Tristan escorted her to the left as Webber continued moving forward until he reached the podium and placed both hands on either edge of the acrylic dais.

"David, thank you," Webber said, shaking hands with his head of Public Relations as they changed places at the podium. "And thanks for warming up the crowd," he added with a wink.

The room suddenly filled with the hum of quiet laughter, but quickly settled down again. Webber smiled and scanned the crowd, nodding to people he knew and trying to make eye contact with as many people as he could. "Before I get started this afternoon, I would like to take this opportunity to thank the KIC Board of Directors: Mr. Scott Mullin, Chief Financial Officer of Restaurant Group South, Ms. Hillary Jordan...." Webber continued introducing each member of the board, accentuating their skills and for whom they worked.

"I would also like to thank Deanna Lynn, my dearest friend and cohort in crime for as long as I can remember." Deanna flashed a huge smile and tilted her head ever so slightly to one side, giving him a coquettish wink. "And last, but certainly not least, my fiancé and best friend, Tristan Moreau." Tristan pressed his lips together tightly and bowed his head. When their eyes met again, Webber saw unconditional love and never-ending support, which warmed him to his core.

Webber turned back to the crowd. "The people standing behind me are much more than just people to me. They are my friends and family as well as colleagues and have shown me nothing but loyalty, respect, and unwavering support from day one." Webber looked over his shoulder and made eye contact with each and every one and mouthed "Thank you." Everyone again responded with a quick nod of their head as Webber once again faced the crowd.

Webber scanned the room. "Now let's get to the first topic on my list of things to cover today," he said, glancing back and forth between his notes and the teleprompter. "For those of you who know me and follow KIC news, you may recognize that one board member is missing from the illustrious group standing behind me. Yes, after seeing the news reports of my personal life, among other things of which he was fully aware, plastered all over the television—and thanks for that by the way," Webber said, flashing his pearly whites as the sound of laughter again filled the ballroom. He paused looking at the crowd, then sarcastically cleared his throat and grinned. "Unfortunately, Mr. Robert Yellos has resigned his position on the KIC board, effective immediately."

There were small gasps and groans from the crowd, and reporters were frantically taking notes as Webber spoke. "I speak on behalf of myself, the current board of directors, and everyone at KIC when I say we all wish you all the best in life and in your future endeavors."

Webber slid a page from one side of the podium to the other and looked up to make sure the teleprompter and his notes were in sync. "Now I'd like to address your reports of my resignation as head of KIC. The short answer is, you were right. I did turn in my resignation to the board a week ago, and before you start taking more notes, it's not for the reasons you reported."

Webber stepped around to the side of the podium, leaned his elbow on the surface, linked his fingers, and crossed his feet at the ankles. "Again for those of you who have followed my career, you know I've been at the helm of KIC since my father died. I, with the help of the board and all of our wonderful and loyal KIC employees, took our small company public and made it what it is today. But with all that success comes a price. Accomplishing as much as we have in such a short period of time has allowed many employees, including me, no time for a personal life, which is why my sexuality—" Webber paused, smiled and winked at the crowd, drawing another rumble of laughter. "—something we'll no doubt get into later, hasn't made it into the spotlight. Until now, that is."

Webber straightened and paced in front of the podium, stopping to look at Tristan before he proceeded. Tristan smiled at him, then at Deanna. Webber watched Deanna slip her hand through Tristan's arm and squeeze, leaving it there in a show of support. He turned back to the crowd and, in an unscripted move, sat on the edge of the stage in front of the podium. "The reason for my resignation is plain and simple. I'm in love and I want a personal life," he said, glancing over his shoulder at Tristan again. "But please make no mistake about it; I will always be involved in KIC. I'm still the major shareholder, and in fact, if the board will have me, I would like to fill Mr. Yellos's seat."

Gasps again filled the ballroom, and people were still scribbling down notes on little pads. Webber stood and walked to the back of the stage. The board, as well as Tristan and Deanna, all looked like they were slightly in shock. "Sorry to spring that on you guys, but I didn't even make the decision until right this second. We can discuss it later, but I wanted it on the table."

Webber walked back to the podium. "Now on to our former chief financial officer, his termination, and the SEC and Justice Department investigations." Webber slid another piece of paper and again checked the teleprompter. "It was brought to my attention by a KIC employee that Mr. Bridges had inflated the price of a particular acquisition by embellishing client lists and fraudulently creating contracts and falsely altering financial documents to support the inflated price. It is alleged that Mr. Bridges split the proceeds with the former owner of the acquisition."

Webber went on to explain to the press that due to poor performance, KIC had divested the company several years later at quite a loss. He also explained how the company was now operating in a new country under a new name and how Nathan had proposed that KIC acquire the same company again, never divulging the company's true identity.

"As soon as this information was brought to my attention, I confronted Mr. Bridges in my office, and he confirmed that our suspicions were correct. He also threatened that if I turned him in, he would drag me down with him by testifying that I was involved in the fraudulent transaction. Fortunately for me, I recorded that conversation, much to Mr. Bridges's surprise, and went directly to the SEC and the Department of Justice."

Webber closed the file, took a deep breath, and again rested his hands on either side of the podium. "So, as you can see, some of your information was accurate, while some was way off base. Yes, there was an SEC and Justice Department investigation, and some of the investigations are still ongoing.

"Regarding my involvement in the matter, I welcomed both agencies to investigate me as well as Nathan, knowing good and well that I had no knowledge of what had gone down. The investigation by the SEC has been concluded, I have been vindicated, and they will not be pressing any charges against me. The Department of Justice has not concluded their investigation, but I'm expecting the exact same outcome. Ladies and gentlemen of the press, I have the truth on my side. But the fact is, I am liable for everything and everyone under my employ. My only mistake was trusting Mr. Bridges. He was an employee of my father and had never given him or me any reason to distrust him. But let me also say that, in my defense, his deception was well done. But as president and CEO of KIC, the buck stops with me. The SEC and the Justice Department have all the proof they need and although I cannot go into details, it appears that there will be an indictment against Mr. Bridges in the very near future. The rest will play out in the courts and there will be justice."

Webber stuck his hand out toward Deanna and Tristan. "Before we conclude, I would like to ask Tristan and Deanna to join me while I clear up the rest of the misconceptions."

Tristan gestured with his hand for Deanna to take the lead, and she sauntered up to the front of the stage with Tristan right behind her. Webber kissed Deanna on the cheek and gave Tristan a quick hug. Deanna stood between the two of them as Webber spoke.

"There has been a good deal of speculation regarding the paternity of Deanna's unborn child. Please—"

Before Webber could continue, Deanna put her hand up. "Please allow me," she said, stepping up to the podium. "As Webber indicated, there has been speculation regarding the identity of the father of my baby. Please allow me to be clear. There has never been a romantic or sexual relationship between Mr. Kincaid and me. We have been the best of friends for many years, and any relationship, besides a sister/brother type relationship, is all hype and fabricated by the press. And although one day I would love to give Webber and Tristan a baby, this one is mine," she said, rubbing her baby bump and smiling. "They're not getting it. Furthermore, I will not divulge the biological father's identity as he does not want to be a part of the baby's life, but I can guarantee without any doubt that it is not Webber Kincaid's baby. Thank you."

Someone shouted a question from the back of the room, and Webber raised a hand. "We will do a short Q&A afterward, but we have one more topic to cover and it involves Tristan and me." Webber took Tristan's hand and brought him up to podium to join him. He smiled at him and began. "Mr. Moreau, Tristan, joined KIC a little over two years ago as my chief administrative assistant. Over those two years, he became quite invaluable to me, and before you start jumping to conclusions, not in the way your dirty little minds are thinking."

Webber winked and looked at Tristan with a wicked smile on his face. Tristan nervously smiled back.

Webber continued, looking back and forth between the crowd and Tristan as he spoke. "Over those two years, we worked very closely together and developed a mutual respect for one another's capabilities. It was during that time that I started to development romantic feeling for him, but we never crossed the line of a boss/subordinate relationship. In fact, we never even knew the other's sexual preference.

"Furthermore, in today's world, with sexual harassments suits, however right or wrong, so prevalent, I would never allow myself to get involved with a KIC employee, especially one who reported to me, for fear of having to explain myself to the board for unacceptable behavior. However, unbeknownst to me, Tristan was experiencing the same types of feelings for me, and because of his strong ethics, he would never put me in that position, so we continued our working relationship while fighting these growing feelings, each of us having no clue about the way the other felt until they were just too difficult to fight."

Webber raised their joined hands. "Obviously, we're together, very happy, and looking forward to starting our lives together."

Webber drew Tristan into a tight embrace. "We did it," he whispered into Tristan's ear, inhaling the smell of Tristan's cologne. Webber then reached over and brought Deanna into the embrace. The crowd roared with applause, and when the noise finally settled, Webber spoke. "Now we'll take a few questions and then we'll allow you to get back to your busy day."

A voice rang out from the back of the room. "Which KIC employee discovered the scam?"

Webber looked out over the crowd to find the source of the question. When he located her, he looked directly at her as he answered. "Unfortunately, we're not at liberty to answer any questions regarding the ongoing investigation. It will all come out in the trial, if and when Mr. Bridges is indicted."

Another voice rose above the crowd. "How could someone pull something like this off without anyone verifying the contracts or the financials?"

"That's a very good question," Webber acknowledged. "The answer is plain and simple. KIC's Finance and Business Development departments are responsible for the due diligence required to totally vet and verify any and all contracts and financials to complete an acquisition. Unfortunately, both of those departments fell under Mr. Bridges's responsibilities. That particular organizational structure is customary and common practice, but KIC immediately rectified the situation and removed the Business Development department from the CFO's responsibilities, and now that department head will report directly to me until my successor is named."

"So Deanna, who's the lucky man who fathered your child?" a voice called out from the front row.

Webber stepped aside as Deanna moved up to the podium and looked in the direction of the voice. She flashed a great big smile as she recognized the reporter from *People* magazine. "Oh come on, Bobby. What part of 'I'm not going to reveal the baby's father' did you not understand?" The crowd roared with laughter.

"Can't blame a guy for trying," the reporter shot back. "But if the father doesn't want you or the baby, I'll volunteer for the job."

"That's very sweet. Bobby, I'll keep that in mind," Deanna said with a wink.

"This question is for the board," a voice yelled from the center of the room.

Since the board had decided that Hillary would speak on their behalf should there be any questions they needed to address, she stepped up to the podium. "Did you ever have any doubt that Mr. Kincaid was involved with Mr. Bridges in this scheme?"

"Never," Hillary said, proudly looking at Webber. "Webber is not only an associate of mine, but a dear friend. I knew Webber's father and I've known him and been on his board longer than any of these guys," she said, looking back over her shoulder. "And I totally trust him and his work ethic. He had nothing to gain from this transaction but money, and from what I can tell, I don't think he needs the money." She smiled at Webber and looked at the crowd for a follow-up.

From somewhere way back in the room, a voice yelled, "What about the fact that Mr. Kincaid used company resources for a pleasure trip he and Mr. Moreau took to the Caribbean that eventually consummated the relationship between him and Mr. Moreau?"

The hairs stood up on the back of Webber's neck. *What in the hell? Who in the hell leaked this?*

Webber realized Hillary was looking at him, waiting for some sort of sign if she should continue or not.

Not sure what else to do but set the record straight, he nodded for her to continue.

She straightened her back and lifted her head as she spoke. "The trip to which you are referring was reviewed by the board and the board deemed it an appropriate business trip. The trip was planned as a working retreat to review possible acquisitions away from the everyday distractions of the company. In fact, that's where it was discovered that one of the acquisitions Mr. Kincaid was considering appeared to be very familiar, which sparked this entire investigation."

Webber's heart stopped because he knew Hillary's statement in his defense would implicate Tristan. He stepped up to the podium but Hillary continued. "In addition, the location of the trip was to property owned by Mr. Kincaid and although he did use the KIC jet, all expenses affiliated with the trip were paid for by Mr. Kincaid personally."

"Thank you, Hillary," Webber said. "That's all the time we have for questions. We appreciate you taking the time out of your very busy schedule to join us today."

Webber turned away from the podium, leading Hillary, when a voice called out. "So that means that Mr. Moreau was the whistleblower?" Webber turned around quickly to see a reporter from CNN he didn't recognize.

He stepped back up to the podium and was about to speak when Tristan joined him, placing his hand on Webber's shoulder. "Let me," Tristan whispered. "The truth will come out eventually. Let's wipe the entire slate clean," he added with a wink.

Webber smiled weakly and stepped aside.

Tristan cleared his throat. "As Mr. Kincaid said earlier, we cannot address the ongoing investigation. But yes, I was the one who first brought to Webber's attention the similarities to a previous KIC acquisition."

Tristan explained how Webber had started tutoring him in mergers and acquisitions and had given him a few completed files to review. He went on to say that the acquisition in question had been one of them. He also explained that the red flags started going up when the client lists and financials rang a bell as being very familiar.

"But," Tristan said, holding up his index finger. "Once we found the original acquisition and compared it to the proposed acquisition, all the pieces of the puzzle fell into place. And as Webber already stated, that's when he confronted Mr. Bridges and contacted the SEC."

"Why did you resign your position from KIC?" another reported asked before Tristan could go on.

"Once Webber and I came forward with our relationship, especially in light of the ongoing investigation, it would have been unethical for me to continue to work in my current capacity. By then Webber had decided that he wanted to take some time to enjoy life and urged me to do the same."

There was a break in the questioning and Webber took advantage of it. "Thanks again. I appreciate the kindness you've shown me over the years, and I hope you'll show the same courtesy to my successor."

With that, Webber took Tristan by one hand and Deanna by the other and followed the board off of the stage and into the adjoining suite, scanning the room. "Where's David?" He yelled.

"Here, sir," David answered, making his way from the door to where Webber was standing. "David, we've got to find the leak."

"Already on it," David replied. "I'm following up on a lead, but I don't think you're going to like it."

"Hell, David," Webber said, releasing Deanna and Tristan's hands and taking David aside, "you've known me long enough to know it doesn't matter if I like something or not. Let me have it."

David hesitated and then leaned in close to Webber's shoulder. "Mr. Yellos," he whispered.

"What?" Webber said through closed teeth.

"One of my sources," David whispered, "who just happens to be a friend of mine, said it was a former board member. He only told me because he's no longer afraid to lose the source since Mr. Yellos resigned from the board."

Webber took a deep breath and looked up at the ceiling. "Thanks, David."

"But sir," David added, "this is a confidential source and I hope you won't implicate him or me."

"I understand," Webber assured him. "I'll keep this on the down low, but I have to share it with the board. Are you comfortable with that?"

"Yes, sir, as long as they know it's confidential."

"Deal. And how many times have I asked you to stop calling me 'sir'?" Webber asked with a smile.

"I know, sir, I'll try."

"That's better, and great job today, by the way."

"Thanks."

Webber walked over to where the board was standing in a huddle, he assumed recapping the press conference. When Webber reached the group, Hillary was the first to speak. "I'm so sorry, Webber, I didn't mean to implicate Tristan," she said, rubbing the back of her neck. "I'll certainly apologize to him as well, but I just wanted you to know."

Webber took both Hillary's hands in his and looked her in the eyes. "Don't give it another thought. The truth was going to come out eventually. In fact, Tristan whispered in my ear when he took the podium that he was happy to get it all out and wipe the slate clean once and for all."

Hillary looked relieved that Tristan had been okay with it but still seemed a little uneasy.

"Look," Webber said, turning to the rest of the board members. "It appears our leak is none other than Yellos."

The board looked stunned. John spoke up. "Seriously?"

"It appears that way."

"How do you know?" John asked.

"David has a contact in the media who confided in him that Bob leaked the details to the press," Webber explained. "But this is confidential, guys," Webber ordered. "We can't blow his source."

"What are you going to do?" John asked.

"I'm not sure yet," Webber confessed. "But he's not going to get away with such unethical behavior. If I have my say, he'll never sit on another board of directors again."

"Just keep us in the loop."

"I promise," Webber insisted.

Six

BACK at home, in comfortable clothing and relaxing in the den, Tristan was seated on the couch with his feet up and Webber's arms draped over his shoulder, both of them sipping glasses of red wine. Deanna was curled up in the big overstuffed chair, covered with a lap blanket, sipping a cup of freshly brewed green tea with the remote in her hand, flipping through the channels. They were waiting for the news coverage of the press conference to start airing, all of them anticipating what type of spin the networks were going to put on the story.

When she hit CNN, she stayed there for a few moments before Tristan heard Webber's name. They cut to a live feed of the CNN reporter at the press conference who asked if Tristan was the whistleblower. Tristan watched himself, as if in slow motion, walk up to the podium, whisper into Webber's ear, and begin to speak. He felt a moment of pride as he told the complete and truthful story to the press. To their credit, CNN aired the remainder of the press conference, and didn't edit sound bites or try to sensationalize the story.

Tristan felt Webber tighten the grip on his shoulder. "You did a really good job up there, Tris," he said. "You might want to think about a future in politics."

"No way," Tristan teased, tilting his head up and giving Webber a slow sensual kiss. When the kiss ended he added, "I'm too honest for politics anyway. Besides, my future is set in stone right here with you."

"Oh God," Deanna said. "Get a room, you two. Do I have to remind you that there is an unmarried pregnant lady present?"

Tristan and Webber both chuckled. Webber stuck his tongue out at her, making a funny face. "You're just jealous that I have a hot man and you don't," he teased.

"Damn straight," she replied. "Oops, my bad. Straight was obviously the wrong word to use."

"Very funny," Tristan snickered, straightening in his seat. "Look, you'll just have to be patient, but we put a man on the moon—I'm sure we can put one on you."

Webber almost spit his wine across the room, and Deanna howled with laughter. "Oh God, that'll go down in the history books. That's why I love hanging out with you 'mo's," she said. "You're so entertaining."

Tristan smiled proudly and sank back down into the couch, feeling pleased with himself.

"'Mo's?" Webber asked with a raised brow.

"Homos," Tristan and Deanna said in unison.

"Ohhhhh," Webber chuckled as he kissed Tristan's temple and snuggled down against him.

The rest of the evening news broadcasts were pretty much the same. As expected, the entertainment news covered Deanna and the baby and Tristan and Webber's coming out, while the financial news covered the investigation and Webber's and Tristan's resignations, with Webber's coming out as a side note.

Tristan lazily opened his eyes when Deanna clicked the television off. Webber stirred and snuggled back against him, apparently not wanting to move. "Let's go to bed," Tristan whispered into Webber's ear, gently lifting him up to a sitting position.

"Goodnight," Deanna said walking over and kissing each of them on the cheek. "Tomorrow morning at breakfast, we can all go over the wedding plans, divvy up the responsibilities, and before you know it, it'll be time for a wedding."

Tristan smiled. "Thanks, Deanna."

Webber stirred again and moaned, mocking Tristan's comment, "Yeah, thanks Deanna."

Deanna smacked him on the head. "You're welcome, asshole."

Webber chuckled, as did Tristan, and just as Deanna turned away, Webber grabbed her hand, pulling her back and kissing her palm. "No really! Seriously, thank you for everything, D."

Deanna ruffled his hair. "I love you too. Goodnight."

THE next two months went by very quickly and without incident. As planned, they'd divvied up the wedding responsibilities, and Deanna and Tristan or Deanna and Webber or all three of them spent at least an hour a day on the phone going over updates, e-mailing constantly, and sharing information. They kept in close contact with the in-house wedding planner at the Inn at Lambert's Cove, giving her information as new developments presented themselves.

On the KIC front, Webber spent a few days a week at the office fulfilling his management responsibilities, although, since his resignation, those were dwindling quickly, allowing him more time to focus on finding his successor. He interviewed over a dozen candidates and had narrowed it down to a final three, whom the board would be interviewing in the next couple of days. This was his last chore before he was more or less free, and hopefully they would make a decision by the end of the week and finally name a suitable replacement.

The wedding was the following Saturday, and he and Tristan planned to meet Deanna on Martha's Vineyard Wednesday afternoon so they could finalize all the last minute details and just relax a day or so before their big day. Tristan had asked if they could go back to the Caribbean on their honeymoon and spend as much time there as they liked with no calendar restraints. Webber had been thrilled with that idea. In his mind, there was no better place to start their new life together.

The previous week, the Department of Justice had called to inform Webber they had concluded their preliminary investigation and, like the SEC, had found him free and clear of any wrongdoing. Once he'd been cleared, Nathan was indicted on several counts of fraudulent behavior, including additional charges of falsifying financial data. He was arrested, booked, and made bail all the same day. KIC's legal team, in conjunction with the SEC and Department of Justice, were all preparing for a lengthy court case in which Webber and Tristan would no doubt have to testify. But if Nathan and his legal team had their way, it would be several years before the case made it to court.

COMFORTABLY seated in the limo on the way to the airport, Tristan looked through a three-ring binder. "Do you think we forgot anything?" he asked, anxiously going over his list.

"Have you seen the back of the limo?" Webber teased. "Let me put this away for you," he said, taking the binder out of Tristan's hand, moving it to his other side, and tucking it between his leg and the car door. "If we forgot anything, we'll just buy it when we get there."

Tristan smirked at the loss of his almighty binder. He'd not let it out of his sight since they'd started planning the wedding. "I just want everything to be perfect."

"And it will be," Webber assured him. "You know why? Because you'll be there and I'll be there and everyone we love will be there."

Tristan sighed. "You're right; I need to stop stressing already."

Webber lifted Tristan's hand and kissed his palm. "That's my boy. By the way, when are Gage and Andy arriving?"

Tristan's nervousness ebbed at the mention of his little brother's name. "Around three o'clock. I can't wait to see them."

"I'm so sorry they didn't make it to Atlanta," Webber shared. "But I totally understand Andy's schedule. Getting called to fill in as backup for Luke Bryan is nothing to shake a stick at."

"Yeah, I'm just glad they're able to make it to the wedding," Tristan admitted. "Andy goes back on tour with Billy Eagan in a couple of weeks."

"That's even more impressive," Webber gushed. "Billy Eagan is the biggest thing in country music these days. I'm really looking forward to meeting them both."

Tristan again started to fidget. "Have you heard from Deanna? Is her flight on time?" he asked nervously.

Webber chuckled. "Tris, you've got to try and relax. And yes, last time I talked to her, they were on time."

"I know, I know. We tried to time our arrivals so if everything went as planned, we would be landing right about the same time."

"Worst case scenario," Webber described very calmly, "if it doesn't go as planned and one of us is delayed, we'll just send another a car for whoever's late."

"Okay," Tristan muttered, laying his head back on the seat and closing his eyes. Webber could see him focusing on his breathing, deeply inhaling and slowing exhaling while trying to calm his jittery nerves.

Webber smiled, still holding Tristan's hand. He turned his head and stared out of the window as the Atlanta scenery went by. His mind started wandering. He felt like he should be nervous—at the very least, a few butterflies should be dancing in his stomach—but he was calm, cool, and collected. It was like he was finally on his way to everything he'd ever dreamed of: his destiny, so to speak. *I resigned my position as head of KIC, sorted through all the shit associated with that, and came out on the other end with the man of my dreams. Why should I be nervous?*

He looked over at Tristan, who was now breathing evenly, and kissed him on the cheek.

Tristan opened his eyes and smiled. He turned his head, which was still resting on the back of the seat. "What was that for?"

"Just because I can," Webber whispered, grinning slightly.

Tristan squeezed Webber's hand, still smiling and gazing into his eyes. "You can do that anytime you like, and anything else you might have in mind, for that matter."

"Don't threaten me with a good time," Webber teased. "Or I will surely take you up on it."

"That's the idea."

The limo came to a stop, and Webber looked out of the window. The driver was getting clearance to drive out onto the tarmac so they could unload the car and board the small jet. Minutes later, they were getting out of the car. They boarded the plane, greeted the flight crew, and were just about to take their seats when Tristan stopped short with a panicked look on his face. "Where's my binder?" he asked with tension in his voice.

Webber lifted his hand and waved the binder in the air. "Got it right here," he said, smiling broadly. He placed the binder on the seat next to Tristan. "Would you like me to sit somewhere else so you and your binder can be alone?" he teased.

When Tristan looked up, Webber saw a flash of hurt in his eyes, and he suddenly felt bad. "Come on, Tris, I was only teasing," he pleaded. "I was just trying to get a laugh out of you."

"It's okay. I know, you're right," Tristan murmured, looking down. "Yes, I'm obsessing again. I feel like I'm back at KIC doing everything in my power to make sure things are perfect for you."

Webber removed the binder from his seat and slid in next to Tristan. "I'm sorry, Tris, I'll behave myself from now on. But it makes me feel worse that you were always under so much pressure at work."

"No!" Tristan said in a shaky voice. "It's not like that at all. I was in love with you, and I couldn't act on that, so the making sure everything was perfect as far as business was concerned was the only thing I could act on. Does that make any sense?"

"Perfect sense," Webber said, looking straight ahead. "And I love you all the more for it. But when I think about all the time we wasted, I want to kick myself in the ass a thousand times."

"Yeah," Tristan admitted. "I want to kick you in the ass a thousand times too."

Shocked, Webber turned to look at Tristan who was now sporting a "cat that ate the canary" look. Webber held up his fisted hand. "Now we're even."

Tristan pressed his fisted hand against Webber's, bumping knuckles and smiling that "gotcha" smile that Webber loved so much.

The pilot spun around in his seat and peeked through the cockpit curtain. "We've been cleared for takeoff, gentlemen. Please buckle up."

THEY touched down on Martha's Vineyard right on schedule and were both surprised to see Deanna standing next to a town car and waving as they taxied in. "Look at her, she's huge," Webber said with an amused tone.

Tristan laughed, punching him in the arm. "You better not say a word about her weight," he warned. "She'll castrate you and that will make for one boring honeymoon."

"You do have a point. How far along is she now?" Webber asked.

"Let's see." Tristan started counting. "She was at the end of her first trimester when we got to the Caribbean, so that's twelve weeks. We were in the Caribbean for three weeks and home over two months, so that should put her just over six months."

"I hope she doesn't explode at our wedding." Webber cringed.

"And… she still has nine to twelve weeks to go if she reaches full term," Tristan added.

The plane came to a stop, and soon after, the attendant opened the cabin door to a bright and sunny New England day.

Tristan felt Webber's hand on the small of his back as they stepped out of the plane. His senses were immediately filled with the same familiar salt air they'd experienced on their first trip. Just before they'd landed, the pilot had given them a weather update. The temperature was hovering at right around eighty-five degrees, with low humidity and winds out of the south at five to ten miles per hour.

"I could get used to this weather," Tristan muttered.

"Me too," Webber agreed. "Maybe we should just buy a place and spend the summers here and the winters in the Caribbean."

"How cool would that be?"

"Very cool. Let's do it."

Tristan looked up and took in the bright blue sky filled with white puffy clouds drifting lazily along. "Are you really serious?"

"Sure, why not?" Webber asked.

"It certainly won't hurt to look," Tristan admitted excitedly. "Maybe we'll find something we just can't live without."

Webber hugged Tristan right there on the tarmac. "Maybe Sam and Cavan can recommend a local realtor."

"Whoa, mister," Tristan protested. "Let's take one step at a time and get this wedding behind us before we add anything else to our to-do list."

"Deal," Webber agreed. "Let's go and say hello to Deanna before she jumps up and down so many times the baby falls out."

"You're so bad," Tristan chastised.

"LOOK at you," Webber said with a smile on his face as they approached Deanna.

She put her hands on her hips and tapped her foot. "One word about my weight, Webber Kincaid, and you'll no longer be a man when you walk up that aisle," Deanna warned.

Webber stopped dead in place. "Ouch," he said with a cringe, instinctively covering his crotch with his hands.

She smiled but didn't stop tapping her foot, apparently waiting for a suitable response.

"Radiant is the only word I can come up with," he said as seriously as he could.

"Aren't I, though," she agreed, curtseying and rubbing her stomach. "Some baby bump, huh?"

"Very impressive," Tristan said, wrapping his arms around her and kissing her cheek. "Webber's right, you're absolutely glowing. Pregnancy sure agrees with you."

She gave him a peck on the cheek. "I'm not sure I agree with either of you, but thanks anyway. The not drinking and not eating sushi is about to kill me, but thank God I'm a natural blonde, 'cause if I couldn't dye my hair for nine months, I'd be hell on heels."

Tristan laughed heartily. "I've missed you," he admitted.

"I've missed you too, honey, and boy do I need to pee."

Tristan looked around for the door to the terminal. "Right this way," he said, linking his arm into hers and leading her toward the door.

Webber watched them walk away, talking a mile a minute as they stepped through the automatic glass terminal doors, not even noticing he wasn't with them. *Well, aren't they as cozy as two peas in a pod. No worries, I'll be right along.*

"Hey, you two, forget anything?" he yelled sarcastically. "It's me, Webber! Remember me?"

He saw Tristan poke his head out of the glass doors. "Stop being so silly. We'll be right back."

Webber smiled, shaking his head in disbelief.

"Where to, sir?" the airport steward interrupted, pushing a cart loaded down with cardboard boxes and suitcases.

"The suitcases can go in the town car with the ladies, and there should be a taxi waiting out front for the boxes," Webber instructed, slipping the steward a twenty-dollar bill.

When Tristan and Deanna reappeared through the terminal doors still arm in arm, Webber jokingly wondered if they'd stopped talking and separated long enough for Deanna to go to the bathroom or if Tristan had joined her in the stall. Seeing their mouths still moving at record-breaking speeds, he'd bet on the latter.

"Did we neglect poor Webber?" Deanna pouted as they walked up to the town car.

"Very funny, D," he whined. "Now get your big baby bump in the car so we can get a move on."

Deanna looked at Tristan. "No, he didn't," she said, swatting at his arm as she climbed into the back of the car. In response, he smacked her on the butt, causing a small squealing sound to escape her lips.

"That'll show you," Webber snarled. He looked at Tristan. "You'd better sit between us," he said, pushing him into the car ahead of him.

"You should be afraid," Tristan said with a chuckle.

WHEN they arrived at the inn, Cavan and Sam, who just happened to be finishing up another wedding tour, greeted them warmly. Sam introduced Tristan and Webber to the potential bride and groom and just as Webber was about to introduce Deanna to the group, the potential groom interrupted.

"You're Miss September. Wait. Don't tell me, ah, Deanna Lynn?" he said matter-of-factly. "That's it. Wow, you're even more gorgeous in person." He turned to his bride-to-be. "Honey, this is one of the supermodels on my *Sports Illustrated* swimsuit calendar."

"I gathered as much," she said rather sharply and stuck out her hand in Deanna's direction. "It's a pleasure to meet you, Ms. Lynn. And I apologize for my babbling future ex-husband."

They all chuckled and Webber watched as Deanna beamed with the attention. "Thank you and no apologies needed. But in case you haven't noticed"—she rubbed her stomach—"you won't catch me anywhere near a swimsuit these days."

"Well, babbling idiot or not, he's right. You are gorgeous."

"Oh stop it, honey, and congratulations, you two," Deanna replied with a slight blush.

The future bride turned to Webber. "And Mr. Kincaid, I'm very sorry to hear about the recent issues with your CFO. I'm a senior VP at Goldman Sachs and I follow KIC quite closely."

Webber was surprised but didn't show it. "Thank you, but it'll all work out. As you probably know, the stock took a bit of a hit but is on its way back up already."

She nodded in agreement. "And where are my manners? I'd like to congratulate you and Mr. Moreau on your upcoming wedding. We really love it here and hopefully, by this time next year, we'll be arriving for our wedding. Once I throw away my fiancé's *Sports Illustrated* swimsuit calendar," she added.

They all chuckled. "Very funny," he said, taking her hand. "Let's let these good folks get settled in."

They said their goodbyes, and Cavan escorted them into the inn while Sam walked the potential bride and groom to their car.

"Ms. Lynn," Cavan said. "We've put you in the Seaside Room, which is right at the top of the stairs, second door on the left."

Webber took her key and her suitcase and led her up the stairs. He unlocked the door and pushed it open for her to enter. "This is lovely," she said as she looked around.

Webber put her suitcase down and took her by the hands. "D, it means the world to me that you're here. We could have never done this without you."

Deanna looked into his eyes. "Tristan is an incredible man, and you're going to have the most wonderful life together," she said, a single tear slipping down her cheek.

"Thank you," Webber said, taking her into an embrace. He finally stepped away, fighting tears himself. "I'll let you get unpacked, and we'll meet downstairs in thirty minutes or so to give you a tour."

"That'll be perfect," she whispered.

Webber stepped out of the room, pulling the door halfway closed before sticking his head back in. "Oh and D." She looked at him with a concerned look. He gestured to the bed. "Tristan and I did it in that bed." Then he gestured to the chair. "Oh, and on that chair too," he added as he quickly closed the door.

"Oh good lord, Webber!" she yelled. "Now where am I going to sleep or sit?"

Webber laughed all the way down the stairs, meeting Tristan at the front desk.

"What's so funny?" Tristan asked, seeming somewhat amused.

"Oh, I had a tender moment with Deanna," Webber explained. "Then ended it by telling her we had sex on the bed and in the chair."

"Webber!" Tristan exclaimed, not able to hold back his grin. "I'll bet she loved that."

"Oh, she loved it alright," Webber agreed. "I think I'll be paying for that one for a while, but I just couldn't help it. She's so easy to tease."

The front door opened and Sam stuck his head inside. "Where do you want all these boxes?"

"Can we put them in the second bedroom of our suite?" Tristan asked. "And sort through it all from there."

"Absolutely. I'll meet you there."

Tristan accepted the key Cavan was dangling in front of him and looked over his shoulder. "We're on our way."

Webber grabbed his suitcase, as did Tristan, and they both made their way outside and around the back of the inn to their suite overlooking the pool area. The room was stunning, decorated in tone-on-tone shades of beige with a partial, heavily fringed canopy covering the bed, and mahogany antique furnishings. There was a living room separating the two bedrooms, each with private baths, and an expansive private deck accessible from either bedroom.

After Sam finished bringing all the boxes to the room, Webber tried to slip him some money, which he refused. "I appreciate it, but it's not necessary," Sam said, pushing his hand away. While Tristan sorted through the boxes, Webber unpacked their bags, putting their toiletries and clothes away, paying special attention to their suits.

Tristan joined him and sat on the foot of the bed. "I can't believe we're really here."

Webber closed the closet door and joined him. "I know. I feel like my entire life has led up to this weekend. I love you, and I'm looking so forward to being your husband."

Their lips met in a heated but unhurried kiss. Webber gently ran his fingers through Tristan's hair as they fell backward onto the bed.

Somewhere in the distance, Webber heard the door slam and someone clearing their throat. He opened one eye and Deanna was standing in the doorway, again with her hands on her hips. "Are you guys going to do it in every room in the inn?" she asked sarcastically, hiding behind a devious grin. "'Cause if you are, I'm changing hotels."

"Party's over," Webber whispered to Tristan, and Tristan chuckled in response.

"I heard that," Deanna said, the grin showing a little more now.

Webber was about to say something snippy when he suddenly realized she was thoroughly enjoying the torture she was bestowing on him. "I think we owe you a tour," he said instead, flashing a huge smile.

Webber couldn't tell if she was surprised or disappointed at his response, but she maintained her stance. "Yes you do," she finally said.

THEY strolled leisurely around the grounds, Tristan and Webber showing her in person everything they'd tried to get her to visualize while they were planning the wedding, without her having actually seen the property. They walked through the pool and patio area where they would have pre-wedding cocktails, the formal gardens where the ceremony would take place, and ended up in the ballroom where they would retire for dinner and dancing after the formal cocktail hour wrapped up.

"This place is perfect for you two," Deanna said, squeezing both of their hands. "I love the fact that it's tucked away from everything and is so private."

Webber noticed a somber look wash over Tristan's face. "What's wrong, Tris?"

"I just hope we can keep it that way," he said, his concerns obvious to them. "So far all the vendors have been sworn to secrecy, but who knows who let what slip. I didn't say anything at the airport, but I saw someone who looked at lot A.J. Hammer, the CNN entertainment news reporter, lurking about."

Webber frowned. "The fact that it's one way in and one way out helps. Starting on Saturday, we have a guard at the entrance, and we can attempt to keep the press out that way."

Deanna took a look around. "We're surrounded by woods, which means anyone could be hanging around out there taking pictures as we speak."

Webber and Tristan instinctively looked around, and then Webber looked up. "I wonder if we can restrict airspace?"

"Not according to the West Tisbury Police Department; I asked," Tristan said. "The only way they will restrict airspace is if it gets too dangerous with multiple helicopters or low-flying aircraft."

"So we take it as it comes," Deanna said. "As long as you two can control your libido long enough to pull the blinds and close the doors, I think we'll be okay. And for everyone's sake, no sex in the pool or hot tub, boys."

Webber and Tristan both laughed nervously. Webber clicked his heels together and saluted Deanna. "Got it, warden."

"Oh stop it, you little shit," Deanna said, swatting at Webber's chest.

"Deanna!" Tristan quipped. "You were so nice and sweet in the Caribbean, and now you've turned into a friendzilla."

Webber put his arm around her. "She's more like Rodan," he said. "But don't get too upset. We've always had this type of relationship."

"Yeah," she said. "He's always needed me to keep him humble. He had everyone in the business world bowing down to him and calling him "king" for way too long. But… I kept him real!"

"I love you," Webber said, drawing her closer, "you witch."

"You two scare me," Tristan said, taking a step away.

Deanna snuggled into Webber's embrace. "You better get used to it, honey, 'cause I don't think it's gonna change any time soon."

"I'll make note of that," Tristan mumbled. "Oh shit," he said, slapping his forehead. "We've got to pick up the marriage license in Edgartown before four o'clock. The law says we have to be in the state of Massachusetts and have the license three days prior to the wedding."

"What time was the rental car being dropped off?" Webber asked.

"I don't know. Someone stole my binder, remember?" Tristan reminded him sarcastically.

Webber rolled his eyes. "Don't get your panties in a wad. It's back in the room."

"I know where it is," Tristan said, proudly lifting an eyebrow. "You think I really let that thing out of my sight? All kidding aside, I think it was scheduled for three thirty. I'll go check with Cavan."

When Tristan rounded the corner to the front of the inn, the rental car was already in the parking lot. He stopped and yelled over his shoulder, "It's already here. Let's get a move on, ladies."

THE next day was spent meeting with the wedding coordinator, the executive chef, the florist, and the justice of the peace, and by the end of the day, they were all exhausted. They sat on the deck outside their room, shoes off and their feet propped on the teak coffee table. Webber and Tristan were sipping a delightful Sancerre and Deanna was nursing a club soda.

"I think everything's done," Deanna confirmed, looking at her boys. "Tomorrow the guests start to arrive, and you have nothing to worry about except greeting them and keeping them entertained until the rehearsal dinner."

"Entertained? Aren't they just going to check in and get familiar with the inn?" Webber inquired. "Oh, and that reminds me, whose job was it to give the turndown gifts to Cavan so they can have them put in each guestroom?"

"It was mine," Tristan volunteered. "And it's done. Deanna did Tiffany proud by retying all the bows around those tiny blue boxes."

Webber nervously took another sip of his wine. "I guess everything is ready then," he said, looking at Deanna and motioning toward the garden.

"Oh," she said, jumping to her feet. "Tristan, I have one question about the flowers on the pergola. Would you walk with me to the garden?"

"Sure," Tristan said. "Web, you want to walk with us?"

"Nah, my feet are killing me," he said, wiggling his toes. "If you don't mind, I think I'll stay right here."

"No problem, we'll be right back."

The minute they were out of sight, Webber jumped to his feet and ran inside to get his telephone. He tapped the screen a few times and lifted the phone up to his ears. After a few rings Webber heard a voice. "Josh White."

"Hi, Josh, it's Webber Kincaid."

"Oh, hey, Webber."

"Everything on schedule?" Webber asked.

"Michael's all set on his end," Josh confirmed. "But he does have a few questions about the type of music your fiancé likes."

"Tristan's favorite artists are Etta James, Dinah Washington, Lena Horne, Frank Sinatra, and, of course, Michael."

"I think Michael can handle that," Josh assured. "We land at four o'clock. That'll give the band time to set up and a little extra time for Michael to do a sound check, as long as you can keep Tristan away from the pool area for a little while."

"That's going to be the hard part," Webber admitted. "Guess what our room overlooks? But I'm going to try to get him to agree to a massage before the dinner."

"Michael only needs ten minutes or so. If he won't agree to the massage, maybe a quick run or something. What time is the grand piano being delivered?"

"It's scheduled for three o'clock, so we should be golden."

Webber heard Deanna talking rather loudly, alerting him to the fact that they were approaching. "Tristan's coming, Josh, I need to go. Call if you have any questions."

"Will do. See you tomorrow."

Webber pressed "End" on his phone just as Tristan and Deanna stepped up onto the deck.

"Who was that?" Tristan asked.

"Well, it was going to be a surprise, but I just booked us a couples' massage tomorrow afternoon."

Tristan's face lit up with joy. That was a sight Webber would never stop trying to recreate over and over again.

"Really?" Tristan said with excitement. "That's just what the doctor ordered. What time?"

"Three o'clock," Webber replied.

"Are you sure we'll have enough time to get back and dressed for the rehearsal?"

"Absolutely," Webber said. "The rehearsal starts at five thirty, cocktails at six, and dinner at seven. We'll have plenty of time."

Tristan bent down and gave Webber a kiss and hugged him tightly. "Thank you."

Webber looked over Tristan's shoulder, winking at Deanna when she gave him the thumbs up.

TRISTAN lay in bed the next morning listening to Webber's slow, even breaths: in and out, in and out. He loved the occasional whimpering sounds Webber made in between breaths and found these stolen moments all very calming. He'd been awake since seven, but he didn't want to chance waking Webber, so he snuggled down in his safe little cocoon and enjoyed the quiet closeness. The day was going to get started soon enough with all the guests starting to arrive, the wedding rehearsal, the caterer setting up for cocktails, and the dinner following. Tristan pulled the covers up over his head and decided to stay in bed as long as he could. But eventually Mother Nature had other plans, and he regretfully slipped out of bed to take care of business. Webber stirred a little but didn't wake. Not wanting to chance waking him, Tristan opted for the deck instead of crawling back into bed. He slipped on the cotton waffle bathrobe the inn provided and looked in the mirror, smoothing his hair on the way to the door.

He slowly eased their guestroom door open, hoping to avoid any cracks or squeaks, and was momentarily blinded by a bright, glorious morning. He shaded his face from the intrusion and slipped out of the room seemingly undetected. When his eyes started to adjust, he was amazed at the beauty of the new day. Rays of bright light were peeking through the gently swaying trees, casting birdlike shadows on the lawn as the sun's rays dried the morning dew. Birds were welcoming the dawn with their morning song as the gardens came to life. Tristan smiled inwardly, feeling like Snow White or Sleeping Beauty in a Disney movie.

A sound distracted him from his revelry, and he turned to see Cavan and Sam's team on the pool deck, guided by the wedding coordinator, already hard at work setting up and arranging tables and chairs for their dinner. The wedding coordinator gave a wave but didn't stop her chores.

He sat in the teak chaise lounge, crossed his feet at the ankles, rested his head back on the chair, and closed his eyes. He listened to the sounds of the morning for the longest time, dozing peacefully and then slowly waking to a new sound. It wasn't long before he felt fingers gently caressing his hair. He opened one eye to a familiar pair of beautiful baby blues staring back down on him.

"Good morning," Tristan whispered. "I hope I didn't wake you."

"Morning," Webber said, sitting at the foot of the chaise. "Are you kidding, I'm too excited to sleep. Besides, it's no fun being in bed without you."

"Flattery will get you everywhere, Mr. Kincaid."

"I was sort of counting on that," Webber responded with that sexy smile that made Tristan weak in the knees.

"Wow," Webber said. "They're already hard at work setting up for dinner."

"Have been since I came out here a little before eight."

Just then, Cavan walked across the pool deck and saw them sitting on the deck.

He waved and smiled. "Good morning, you two. Looks like it's going to be a beautiful day."

They both waved back, nodding their heads in agreement. "It sure looks that way," Webber answered.

"I'd love to stop and chat," Cavan said with humor in his voice. "But in case you didn't know, we have a wedding here this weekend. Lots to do."

Tristan and Webber laughed. "That's what we heard," Tristan replied as Cavan continued past them, apparently on the way to his next chore.

"I think we should get back in bed and treasure the last moments of quiet we have until after the wedding," Webber suggested.

"Why, Mr. Kincaid, are you trying to lure me back into your bedroom to have your way with me?"

"Damn straight," Webber said, standing and offering Tristan his hands.

"Okay, then," Tristan replied as Webber pulled him to his feet. "Just so I know."

WHEN Tristan and Webber reemerged a couple of hours later, the patio had been transformed into a poolside dinner club. Four round tables seating six guests each were covered in seafoam-green linen underlayments with ivory toppers and seafoam-green runners and matching napkins. Deanna was busy arranging place cards while the wedding coordinator was overseeing the delivery of the centerpieces. Tristan and Webber leisurely rested on the handrail, admiring the scene as the florist carried in the first of four large centerpieces. Each one was about three feet tall and featured large magnolias surrounded by pastel-colored flowers in various shades of green spilling over the top of tall thin vases. There was an area for the band, a dance floor tucked away in the corner, and a bar on the opposite side of the tables. There were tiki torches surrounding the pool area and large magnolias floating throughout the pool.

"It's going to be beautiful tonight with everything all lit up," Tristan said to Webber.

"Magical," Webber replied. "Just like you," he added, kissing Tristan on the cheek.

"Get a room," Deanna yelled from the patio.

Webber and Tristan waved and made their way down to her.

"Should you be on your feet this much?" Tristan asked Deanna as she floated around with place cards in her hand.

"I'm really enjoying myself," she replied. "I do believe when the runway turns on me, I've got another career in wedding planning."

"If this is any indication," Webber said, "I think you're right. This looks fabulous."

"Thanks and I agree, if I do say so myself."

"Stop for a little while and come with us to get some breakfast," Tristan urged. "You need to eat."

"By the size of me, one would think eating is all I'm doing," she teased.

"Seriously, this will all be here when we get back," Tristan said, gesturing to their surroundings.

"I guess I could use a bite."

"COME on, Tris, the shuttle is going to be here any minute," Webber called from the deck.

"On my way," he yelled. "You can't greet your guests with your hair sticking up all over the place, ya know."

Webber had to laugh. That was typical Tristan. On the way back from breakfast, they'd stopped and taken a walk along Lambert's Cove beach. The sun was high in the sky and making the water sparkle like a pool of emeralds. There was a brisk breeze, and the salt air was fresh and abundant. They'd all agreed it felt wonderful having the sand under their feet, but the minute they'd returned, Tristan and Deanna ran for their rooms to tidy up before the guests started arriving.

Tristan and Webber had chartered a small jet to bring everyone from Atlanta, which was his five board members and their spouses, along with Sophie and her husband. They'd also flown in Kenton, Amani, and Kit from Nectar Island, and Gage and Andy from Nashville. Although Gage had convinced Tristan to invite the rest of his family, the invitations had gone unanswered. So with Deanna, the entertainment, the wedding coordinator, whom Webber and Tristan had insisted be seated at a table, Cavan and Sam, and the two of them, the guest list topped out at twenty-four. It was everyone that meant anything to them and they were happy to have them all there.

The screen door slammed and Tristan popped out looking like a million bucks. "Worth the wait?" he asked.

"Absolutely! You look good enough to eat."

"I'll remember that later," Tristan said with a gleam in his eyes. "Come on, what are you waiting for?"

Just as they rounded the corner of the main house, the chartered shuttle was entering the parking lot. When the shuttle came to a stop, Sophie was the first one out. She threw herself into Webber's arms and then Tristan's, her husband Tony right behind her with her purse and tote bag. Next off the shuttle were Hillary and Paul Jordan, Scott and Amy Mullin, Cynthia and Bill Bowen, Betty and Ira Katz, and, last but not least, John Reynolds and his partner Charles Winthrop.

Webber opened his arms and looked around, gesturing to his surroundings. "Welcome to the Inn at Lambert's Cove."

He looked at Tristan and smiled. "Tristan and I are so happy you all were able to join us for our special weekend. You'll never know how much it means it us."

Tristan joined his hands and looked back and forth between Webber and their guests. "Cavan and Sam are waiting inside to get everyone checked in, and there are some refreshments inside to tide you over until dinner. If you need anything at all, please don't hesitate to ask."

Before everyone could get inside, a sedan pulled into the parking lot. "It's Gage and Andy," Tristan said excitedly.

The car waited at the entrance while the shuttle bus turned around, and Tristan bounced on the balls of his feet in anticipation of seeing his brother. Webber suddenly felt a lump in his throat and tears stinging the backs of his eyes when he realized just how much it meant to Tristan to have his brother here.

The car finally pulled up to the walkway and came to a stop. When Gage stepped out, Webber only got a glimpse of his soon-to-be brother-in-law before Tristan was throwing his arms around him and hanging on for dear life. From what Webber could see, Gage was a rougher, younger version of Tristan. Same hair, same eyes, and same build. Gage was a little thicker and bulkier than Tristan, obviously from ranch work, but they could have been twins.

Andy stepped out of the car right after Gage, and he and Webber stared at each other for a moment before Andy rolled his eyes. "It's like this every time they get together," he said to Webber. "I'm Andy White. You must be Webber."

"Guilty as charged," Webber said, offering his hand. He went on playfully, "How long will this go on?"

"Oh, who knows," Andy replied. "Gets worse the longer they go without seeing one another."

"We can hear everything you guys are saying," Tristan said, stepping back but keeping his arm flung over Gage's back.

"Gage, this is Webber."

Gage stuck his hand out to shake, but Webber stepped up and threw his arms around Gage's shoulders. "Good to meet you, Gage. I've heard a lot about you."

"Likewise," Gage said, sounding startled.

Webber stepped back and raised an eyebrow. "Really? You'll have to share a little of that with me."

"I've been sworn to secrecy," Gage replied with a wink. And then he mouthed "I'll tell you later."

"I saw that," Tristan said, punching his brother in the arm.

"Okay, all this is well and good and I love you all, but I need a beer," Andy said.

"Oh man, where are our manners," Webber said gesturing inside. "Let's get you guys something to drink."

They escorted Gage and Andy inside where Cavan and Sam were still checking the first round of guests in, so they showed them to the bar for a beer and snacks.

Webber noticed through the windows that another car was pulling up the drive. "Must be the Nectar Island crew," he said to Tristan.

Tristan looked torn between leaving his brother and going with Webber to greet Kenton, Amani, and Kit, but he knew it was the right thing to do. "We'll be right back. Guys, we have one more carload of guests to greet."

Webber and Tristan walked out of the front door hand in hand as Kit jumped out of the car. She ran up the walk, flying into Webber's arms. Webber released Tristan's hand and swung her around. He put her back down while hugging her tightly and kissing her on the cheek. "You look great, Kit," Webber said. "How's life treating you?"

"Oh, you know, the usual, but we'll have time for that later," she offered as she flew into Tristan's arms, wrapping her arms around his neck and whispering in his ear. "Tristan, I'm so happy for the two of you."

"Thanks, Kit," he said, squeezing her tightly and then holding her at arm's length. "It's so good to see you. You're beaming. Is there something you need to tell us? I do believe I detect a twinkle of love in those green eyes."

Kit blushed and lowered her head but then looked up at him through her lashes. "Maybe," she whispered. "I can't wait to tell you all about him."

Webber covered his ears. "I don't want to hear this, not for another ten years."

Kit swatted Webber on the arm. "Oh Webber, you're never going to let me grow up."

"If I have my way, you won't ever grow up," he said, feeling a little old and weary.

Suddenly, Amani appeared in front of him, looking a little teary-eyed. "Mr. Webber, it sure is good to see you." She threw her arms around him and pulled him against her full figure in a crushing embrace. Then, she turned to Tristan. "You too, Mr. Tristan."

Kenton pulled up the rear, shaking Webber's and Tristan's hands while trying to balance Amani's and Kit's purses and totes.

"Good to see you, Kenton. How's everything on Nectar Island?"

Kenton smiled proudly. "Everything's just fine, sir. No news to report."

"No news is good news," Webber said, leading them into the inn.

Webber saw Tristan nervously looking around, he assumed for Gage and Andy. "Why don't you go and find the boys while I get the rest of our guests checked in and to their rooms?" he offered.

Tristan's eyes lit up. He kissed Amani and Kit on the cheek and promised to see them shortly.

"Don't forget we have appointments in a little while," Webber reminded him with a slight grin.

"I won't," Tristan promised as he ran out the front door.

TRISTAN found Gage and Andy seated on chaise lounges that had been moved across the pool deck so they could set up for dinner.

"Sorry about that," he said, taking a seat at the foot of Gage's chair, forcing Gage to move his booted feet.

"Have a seat, why don't you?" Gage teased.

"Shut up."

Gage smiled broadly. "It sure is good to see you, big bro."

Tristan laid his hand on Gage's leg. "You too," he said genuinely, looking back and forth between them. "You guys really look great."

"So do you," Andy added with a wink. "Love agrees with you."

"I don't know about how I look," Tristan replied, "but I'm really happy."

"Webber seems really nice," Gage said, looking at Tristan. "I'm not sure what I was expecting, but he wasn't it."

Tristan raised an eyebrow. "What were you expecting?"

"Like I said, I'm not sure. Maybe someone a little more egotistical or uptight."

"Why would you think that?" Tristan asked, tilting his head to one side.

"I don't know," Gage mused. "A lot of people in his position, you know, rich and powerful, are pretty full of themselves."

"Well that couldn't be further from the truth where Webber's concerned," Tristan assured. "He's the most grounded person I know."

Andy reached over and squeezed Tristan's leg. "We're really looking forward to getting to know him."

Gage interrupted. "So no word from Mom and Dad, huh?"

Tristan looked down at his feet and shook his head. "No. I really didn't expect them to come, but I at least thought Mom would call or something."

Gage didn't answer, and Tristan knew that whenever Gage didn't have a smartass comment, he was struggling with something.

"Ok," Tristan said, looking into Gage's eyes. "Spill it."

"You know I hate to get in the middle of the drama," Gage said, apparently not wanting to reopen a gaping wound.

"I know. Never mind," Tristan murmured.

He must have sounded somewhat defeated because Gage moved his chair to an upright position and crossed his arms over his chest.

"Mom wanted to call, but Dad forbade it. There, I've said it."

"I figured as much," Tristan replied.

"Look, Tristan," Gage said sympathetically, "I don't agree with how she's handling things, but she's in a tough position. She loves you, but you helped put her husband and oldest son in jail."

"I had no choice, Gage, you know that," Tristan reiterated. "I was subpoenaed. What could I do, lie under oath? Besides, they had all the information they needed to convict them before I even went to work there. The only reason they put me on the stand was to make sure the jury saw that a family member was testifying against them so they would get a conviction."

Gage leaned back and was now looking up at the trees, obviously contemplating his next words. When he spoke, it was barely a mumble. "Tristan, I don't blame you, but I wish like hell you'd never gone to work there. It ruined our family."

Andy reached over and put his hand on top of Gage's in an apparent show of support.

Tristan laid his hand on top of theirs. "I know. I wish for that every day of my life, but I can't change the past. If they can't see that I had no choice, then I can't worry about what I can't control."

Gage nodded.

"Come on, Gage," Tristan tried to explain as calmly as possible, "I've decided I'm not reaching out to them anymore. I'm done. You have them, Andy and his family, me, and now Webber. All I have are you guys and Web, but I think that's enough for me, for now. But eventually Web and I are going to start our own family, and I hope you guys will choose to be part of it."

Gage looked at Tristan and smiled. "You guys are gonna have kids?"

"I think so. I mean we haven't decided for sure, but we've talked about it."

"Good for you," Gage said, laughing. "I think you'll make a great mommy."

Tristan punched Gage in the arm.

"Ouch!" Gage yelled, grabbing his arm. "That hurt."

"Serves you right, I'll show you what kind of mommy I'm gonna make."

Tristan watched as Gage's features softened. "Of course we'll be part of your family, but you can't blame me for trying to put mine back together."

"I don't blame you, but at some point, you've got to see that it just won't work. They hate me, and I guess in their minds, they have a right. But I'm not the bad guy. How long am I supposed to try and reach out to them just to have them reject me again and again? It hurts, Gage, and I'm tired of it."

Gage leaned up and placed both is hands on Tristan's shoulders. "You're right. But I'm always in the middle, and I just wanted—"

"I know what you want, Gage, and it kills me that I'm the reason you can't have it. But I'm through beating myself up for it; it's time for me to let it go."

Gage nodded again. "It's okay. I'm a big boy now and I can deal, but I'll never stop wanting my family back together again."

"And that's okay too," Tristan said. "But wishing and hoping doesn't always make it happen. Trust me, I know. I spent a lot of long hard years learning that lesson."

Tristan saw movement out of the corner of his eye and turned to see Webber coming through the pool gate. He squeezed Gage's leg again. "I love you, little brother, and thanks for being here."

"I'm sorry if I'm interrupting," Webber said as he walked up, resting his hand on Tristan's shoulder. "But we have that appointment we have to get to, remember?"

Tristan looked up and smiled. "Not interrupting, just catching up is all. And of course I remembered."

"Well, gentlemen," Webber said. "Can I steal this man for a little while?"

"Please do," Gage said, kicking Tristan off of his chair. "Maybe now I can enjoy the rest of my beer in peace."

Tristan looked over at Andy. "He's such a smartass. How do you put up with him?"

"I don't know," Andy teased. "Great in bed maybe?"

"Thanks," Gage said, looking quite proud of himself.

"Whoaaa," Tristan whined. "TMI, bro, T. M. I."

Webber seemed to enjoy Gage's antics, and that warmed Tristan more than he'd expected. He so wanted Webber, Gage, and Andy to get along well. These guys were all the family he had, and he needed them all.

WHEN Webber and Tristan returned from their massage, the pool area was completely transformed. The tables were all set with beautiful gold-rimmed china with matching gold-rimmed crystal stemware. The dinner napkins were decoratively folded and hanging half off the end of every place setting with a place card indicating the guest to be seated there.

Leaning on the handrail overlooking the pool, Tristan stared in amazement at how the area had been transformed since they'd left just under two hours ago. He noticed the new addition of a beautiful, shiny black grand piano surrounded by a saxophone on a stand, a full set of drums, a bass, and several microphone stands. Webber slipped his arms around Tristan's waist and rested his chin on Tristan's shoulder. "Beautiful, isn't it?" Webber whispered.

Tristan nodded then turned within Webber's embrace and kissed him slowly. When the kiss ended, Tristan sighed. "I can't ever remember being this happy," he said.

Webber flashed a concerned smile. "I'm so glad to hear that. When I interrupted you and Gage, it looked like you guys were into something very pretty heavy, and I was afraid something was wrong."

"With us?" Tristan asked. "No way. It's just, well, I decided that I'm giving up on ever having any type of relationship with my parents. I'm tired of reaching out time after time and them shunning me. And Gage… well, he really wants us to be a family again, but I can't do that alone."

"How long have you been thinking about all of this?" Webber questioned.

"That's the thing. I haven't really thought about it, at least not consciously. But I feel badly that Gage is caught in the middle of all this. All he really wants is to have his family back, but when he asked if I'd heard anything from my parents, it all just hit me. I no longer cared if they loved me or not."

"Tris," Webber whispered. "I'm sorry."

"Don't be. I feel lighter somehow, like I've let it go and it's a great feeling. I guess I didn't realize how much all this was weighing on me."

Tristan saw the concern in Webber's crystal-blue eyes.

"You didn't ask for any advice, so I'm only going to say this. Just let it be for a while and don't close any doors permanently."

"I always want your advice, and I'll think about what you said, but it feels so good not to wonder if they'll ever speak to me again. It's almost like I took the power to hurt me away from them. I can't believe it took me all these years to figure that out."

Webber pulled Tristan into another embrace. "I'll support you in any decision you make. You know that, right?"

"Yes, I've always known that, and I love you for it. But you know what?" Tristan said.

"What?"

"We're getting married tomorrow, and all of the people that matter most to us are here. That's more than enough for me."

"If it's good enough for you, then it's good enough for me."

Webber looked down at his watch. "Oh geez, it's five o'clock. We've got thirty minutes to get ready for the rehearsal."

"Then we better get a move on," Tristan replied, ending the statement with a quick kiss.

THE actual rehearsal went very quickly, and in no time Webber and Tristan were mingling with their guests, light jazz, conversation, and laughter filling the predusk air. If Tristan thought the place was magical in the daylight, he couldn't find any words to describe how it looked in the dusk. With all the torches, votives, and pool candles lit and the soft music filling the night, the area took on an air Tristan could only describe as the most magically romantic scene he'd ever experienced.

Before he knew it, cocktail hour was over, and he and Webber were seated for dinner at a table with Deanna, Gage, and Andy. Lobster bisque and a grilled peach and roasted beet salad preceded the entrées of rack of lamb or pan-roasted Chilean sea bass. Dinner was superb, and the servers were now dropping off molten chocolate lava cake with whipped cream, strawberries, and a lit sparkler dazzling each dessert.

The band stopped and Webber took Tristan by the hand and led him up to one of the microphones. "On behalf of Tristan and me, I would like to thank everyone for making the journey to this beautiful island to witness our special day." Everyone broke out in loud applause, and Webber leaned over and stole a quick kiss while the guests settled down. "I have a big surprise for all of you," he said, "but especially for Tristan. Everyone, please welcome Mr. Michael Bublé."

Tristan's mouth hung open in disbelief. *Did Webber just say Michael Bublé?* He watched the silhouette of a man enter the pool gate and walk up to the microphone. *It is Michael Bublé!*

Tristan was speechless as Michael took his hand and then Webber's. "Congratulations to you both," he said and then looked at the band as he raised his hand and then dropped it. The band started the intro to a song Tristan immediately knew as "For Once in My Life."

Webber took him by the hand again and dragged him to his seat, Tristan's mouth still gaping open from the shock of it all.

"How, when?" he whispered, almost speechless.

"Anything and everything for you," Webber said, squeezing his hand tightly.

"Thank you" was all Tristan could say before the tears started running down his cheeks.

Webber brushed the tears away with his thumbs and kissed him. "Just sit back and enjoy the show."

When Michael's first set ended, Tristan was on his feet, yelling and clapping feverishly along with the rest of the guests. Michael took another bow and stepped away for a short break before starting his last set.

SECONDS later, Webber heard a clinking noise and looked over his shoulder to see Deanna tapping a knife against her water glass. "Can I have everyone's attention?" she asked, still clinking.

The crowd began to settle until eventually all that could be heard was the crickets through the silence of the night. Deanna walked up to the microphone with her water glass in hand.

Webber turned to Tristan and smiled.

"As most of you know, I'm Deanna Lynn, the beautiful, talented, and used-to-be slim swimsuit and runway supermodel and just an all-around knockout," she said rubbing her belly and winking at the crowd, which drew a roar of laughter.

"I'm also Webber's best woman, best girl, or whatever the hell you call it these days," she added, waving her hand in the air. "And one of my jobs is to say a few words about him. And boy have I been itching to do that for as many years as I can remember."

"Oh geez," Webber mumbled, looking at Tristan and drawing another burst of laughter from the guests.

She paused and smiled coyly at Webber and then looked out over the crowd. She began again. "If you read the tabloids, you all know that Webber and I have been romantically involved for many years, and he's the suspected father of my unborn child." She rolled her eyes and paused for effect. "Not!" she added with a giggle.

"And, according to the national news, I'm devastated that the handsome and wicked Tristan Moreau stole my man right out from under my feet. Uh... do I look devastated to you?" she asked, looking out over the crowd while rubbing her belly again. "Wait, don't answer that.

"But seriously, Webber and I have been best friends and confidants for so long, I can't remember him not being in my life. We've gotten each other through some of the hardest times, including him almost screwing up this relationship and letting this incredible man slip through his fingers." She looked down at Tristan and smiled. "But I saved them both from destruction. Yes, you're welcome," she teased, nodding at each of them. "In fact, just so you'll know how much I love my guys, I recently asked them to be the godparents of my baby."

The guests were immediately on their feet and applauding. When they settled down again, she continued. "They are entering into this marriage with a solid foundation of mutual love and respect, and if anything ever happened to me, I can't think of anyone else I'd want to raise my child. Webber and Tristan, I love and respect you both so much, and I wish you all the happiness in the world. Love one another, support one another, cherish every moment you have together, and you'll be happy for a lifetime."

Before anyone could react to Deanna's closing comments, a loud voice interrupted the silence.

"Bravoooo! Bravoooo! Now isn't that sweet?" a voice said from beyond the fence.

When the silhouette of a man approached the gate, Webber immediately recognized the swagger. "Oh shit, it's Nathan Bridges," he whispered.

The guests were now silent, all looking in the direction of the voice.

"What?" Tristan asked. "Are you sure?"

"Oh yes, I'm sure," he guaranteed. "Get out of here and call 911."

"No! Webber, I'm not leaving you."

Webber opened his mouth to speak, but quickly remembered what he'd promised Tristan weeks ago about not trying to protect him. "Damn," Webber said, looking around.

"Deanna," he said in a very low voice.

She looked his way and he motioned for her to join him. "Who is that?" she asked.

"It's Nathan Bridges," he explained. "Can you please go through the other gate to the front door and call 911?"

"Okay," she replied in an uneasy voice. Webber followed her as she safely made her way across the pool deck and through the gate.

Gage must have seen her, because he was right on her heels, which made Webber feel a little better.

Webber studied Nathan as he approached the gate and saw him step through with an almost empty bottle of Jack Daniels in one hand and a handgun in the other. As soon as the crowd saw the gun there were gasps and incoherent rumbles of low voices.

Webber stood up and walked toward Nathan. "That's far enough, Nathan. The police are on their way."

Nathan stopped, swaying back and forth. He took a swig from his bottle and made a face as the bourbon slid down his throat. "I won't need much time," he slurred. He held an unsteady hand up, pointing the gun at Webber. "You ruined my life and now you're going to pay."

"No!" Tristan yelled, running up and standing in front of Webber. "It's me you want. I'm the one who brought all this to Webber's attention."

"Tristan!" Webber screamed. Frantic to put a stop to all of this, Webber turned his attention back to Nathan as he pushed Tristan aside. "You don't want to do this, Nathan. Either way you're going to jail, but I think it would a lot less time if you weren't convicted of murder."

"Enough, Webber! Do you think I'm that stupid? I don't intend to ever go to prison, but when I die, you and your little boyfriend here," he said, waving the gun back and forth, "are going to be there to greet me."

Webber looked around quickly for anything that might help them. He caught movement out of the corner of his eye and saw Gage sneaking up behind Nathan. *He must have gone around the front. Good man, Gage. Stall. I've got to stall to give him some time.*

"Look, Nathan," Webber pleaded. "You asked me to testify on your behalf. If you let Tristan go, I'll do it. I'll say it was one big misunderstanding. I'll get the charges dropped."

"Too little, too late," Nathan hissed. "You and your boy toy are history." He pointed the gun at Webber and pulled the trigger. Tristan threw himself in front of Webber just as Gage tackled Nathan. The crowd screamed in horror as the gun went off and Tristan and Webber fell to the ground.

Cavan and Sam rushed Nathan, who was fighting Gage for the gun, while Andy ran to Tristan and Webber. The other men in the crowd followed suit, and in a couple of minutes, Nathan's hands were secured behind his back by Gage's belt and Kenton was sitting on top of him.

As the sirens wailed in the distance, Webber froze, holding Tristan tightly, not wanting to let him go. "Tristan?" he asked. No answer. "Tristan, can you hear me. Are you hurt?"

Tristan mumbled something that Webber couldn't make out. "Say it again, baby. Are you hurt?"

"I-I can't breathe."

Panic ran through Webber's veins. *Oh Jesus, please don't take him from me.*

He heard Tristan trying to speak again. "Let me go, I can't breathe."

Webber released him and Tristan started moving, gasping for air, but moving. "I'm alright," he said. "You were holding me so tight I couldn't breathe."

Andy helped Tristan to his feet and then Webber. "I'm okay," Tristan said. "The bullet didn't hit me."

Webber took Tristan into his arms again, some of the fear slowly dissipating. "If you ever do anything like this again, I'll kill you myself."

"Oh stop being dramatic. You're not going to kill me."

"No, but *I* will," Gage said as he rushed Tristan and threw his arms around his brother.

"Both of you," Tristan said, "get a grip. We're all okay."

The entire episode from the time Nathan showed up until the police took him away lasted less than fifteen minutes. Being escorted to the police car in handcuffs, Nathan vowed to get even with them one day, and Webber was sure he meant it. If Nathan ever got out of prison, they'd have to watch their backs.

WEBBER and Tristan walked up to the microphone, brushing off their clothing, and apologized to their guests for the unwanted intrusion. "Please," he begged. "Don't let Nathan ruin this special night. Let's enjoy our time here."

Everyone returned to their seats and Michael was kind enough to return to the stage for the second half of his show and even cracked a few jokes about how next time he was wearing a bulletproof vest and how dangerous it was performing on Martha's Vineyard.

The evening ended with a final toast from Gage. "I'm Gage Moreau, Tristan's little brother, and if you would have asked me how this night would have gone, I don't think I could have ever made up such a story, but...." He looked directly at Tristan. "I'm so proud of you, bro. Always have been, always will be."

He moved his gaze to Webber. "It's so obvious how deep your love is. You were both willing to risk your lives for the other and that, I guess, says it all. Webber, welcome to the family."

Gage smiled at Andy and then the crowd. "I'm so lucky to have Andy in my life and now Tristan has Webber. I know I speak for everyone when I wish you nothing but happiness and love. I love you guys."

Seven

THE next afternoon was glorious as the guests accompanied Tristan and Webber down the aisle following the bluesy jazz sounds of the Olympia Brass Band. When the crowd reached the pergola, everyone took their seats, leaving Webber and Deanna, Tristan and Gage, and the justice of the peace standing before the crowd.

"Good afternoon," the officiant said. "We are gathered here today, not to witness the beginning of what will be, but rather what already is! We do not create this marriage, because we cannot. We can and do, however, celebrate with Tristan and Webber and their friends and families the wondrous and joyful occurrence that has already taken place in their lives."

She paused, smiling at Tristan and Webber, then looked out over the crowd.

"Marriage is a supreme sharing of experience and an adventure in the most intimate of human relationships. It is the joyous union of two people whose comradeship and mutual understanding have flourished into romance. Today Tristan and Webber proclaim their love and commitment to the world, and we gather here to rejoice, with and for them, in the new life they now undertake together.

"The joy we feel now is a solemn joy, because the act of this marriage has many consequences, both social and personal. Marriage requires love, a word we often use with vagueness and sentimentality. Tristan and Webber, this celebration is the outward token of your sacred and inward union of hearts. It is a union created by your loving purpose and kept by your abiding will. It is in this spirit and for this purpose that you have come here to be joined together.

"Who holds the rings?"

"I do," Deanna said, opening her palm and revealing two rings, the one Webber gave to Tristan when he proposed and an identical one he'd purchased for himself.

The officiant held out her hands, and Deanna placed both rings in her palm.

"These are the rings that Tristan and Webber will wear for the rest of their lives, which express the love that they have for one another. These rings are circles, symbols that remind us of the Sun, the Earth, and the universe. Symbols of holiness, of perfection and peace that have no beginning and no end. And so, in this moment, let us all bring our blessings to these rings to also be symbols of unity, of joining and of commitment. Tristan and Webber, will you please face each other and join hands."

Tristan and Webber joined their hands and gazed into one another's eyes.

The officiant continued. "As you state your vows to one another, be mindful of the love around us represented by our family and friends. Tristan?"

Tristan's body tingled from head to toe and his hands were shaking slightly, but he felt Webber's strong grip keeping him steady. He looked straight into Webber's eyes, cleared his throat, and attempted to say the words filling his heart.

"Webber," he said, his voice a little shaky and his hands trembling as he took the ring from the officiant's hand and placed it on Webber's finger halfway. "We entered into each other's lives with no intention of finding love in the confines of the workplace. But what we found was so much more than love. Almost from the first day we met, I felt this overwhelming attraction to you. At first I kept telling myself it was nothing more than awe, admiration, and respect for what you'd accomplished in your life, but even then I think I knew I was lying to myself. It wasn't until you took me under your wing and we began to work so closely together that I allowed myself to accept that what I was feeling was so much more. I'd fallen in love with you. After cursing myself a thousand times and swearing that nothing would ever come of it, I accepted that fact and did what I could do, under the cloak of my job, to make sure you were always taken care of. The weight of my love for you felt like it might crush me sometimes, but my only option was to leave and I could never do that of my own free will. So I stayed and worshipped from afar. Until everything I'd ever dreamed of came to me—you! You took a leap of faith and came to me with your heart in your hands, telling me you felt the same way I did. My heart was and is so full of love for you, I'm afraid sometimes it might just burst open. I love you with every fiber of my being and with every beat of my heart. I love you, Webber, now and always."

Tristan closed his eyes, took a deep breath, and pushed the ring the rest of the way onto Webber's finger. When he opened his eyes, he saw the tears threatening to spill from Webber's baby blues, and he squeezed Webber's hands, hopefully giving him the reassurance that he felt the same way.

WEBBER knew his palms were sweating as he released Tristan's hands and took the other ring from the officiant's hand. Tristan's words filled his heart and soul, making them soar to places they'd never been. He struggled to keep his legs sturdy under him as he slipped the ring on Tristan's outstretched hand. He took a deep breath and began to speak.

"Tristan, until I met you, my work was my life. In many ways it was my partner as well. I, too, fought the feelings that developed so quickly. For two long years, I found excuses to stop by your office to chat, to share coffee and a cheese danish in the mornings, and yes, I even changed my gym schedule to work out with you, until you changed yours to avoid me," he said with a slight grin.

Tristan smiled and Webber knew he'd busted him even though Tristan had never confirmed his suspicions.

Webber continued. "I was in the horrible position of being in love with you and not being able to do anything about it. Then I made the unconscious decision to take action and follow my heart instead of my head, and it turned out to be the best decision of my life. I've never felt about anyone the way I feel about you. You fill my heart with so much love that sometimes it hurts. You calm and nurture me, and you make the hard stuff in life so much easier to take. You are a part of me that I will never let go and never ever be able to live without. To just say 'I love you' is not nearly enough. Nothing can adequately describe my feelings, emotions that run so deep they can never be revealed by mere words. I promise to spend the rest of my life showing you how much I love you each and every day."

Webber slipped the ring over Tristan's knuckle as he blinked back tears.

The officiant nodded. "Tristan, will you take this man, whose hands you hold, choosing him alone to be your lawfully wedded husband? Will you live with him in the state of true matrimony? Will you love him, comfort him, through good times and bad, in sickness and in health, honor him at all times, and be faithful to him?"

"I will," Tristan said.

"Webber, will you take this man, whose hands you hold, choosing him alone to be your lawfully wedded husband? Will you live with him in the state of true matrimony? Will you love him, comfort him, through good times and bad, in sickness and in health, honor him at all times, and be faithful to him?"

"I will," Webber said.

The officiant continued. "Tristan and Webber, remember to treat both yourselves and each other with respect, and remind yourselves often of what brought you together. Give the highest priority to the tenderness, gentleness, and kindness that your connection deserves. When frustration, difficulty, or fear assail your relationship—as they threaten all relationships at one time or another—remember to focus on what is right between you, not only the part that seems wrong. And if each of you takes responsibility for the quality of your lives together, your life together will be marked by abundance and delight.

"In as much as you have consented together in this ceremony to live in wedlock and have sealed your vows in the presence of this company and by the giving of these rings, it gives me great pleasure to pronounce that you are now one."

The officiant looked out into the crowd. "I present to you Tristan and Webber Moreau-Kincaid. You may kiss your groom."

Webber pressed his lips lightly onto Tristan's and felt everything he'd ever wanted and would ever want in the future all wrapped up into one. He felt Tristan's arms around him tightly as he returned the kiss. Before either of them could say anything, all the guests gathered around them with hugs and words of congratulations. The Olympia Brass Band started a jazzy version of the Wedding March and led the procession back down the aisle together.

AS THE night came to an end, Tristan and Webber stood hand in hand in the foyer saying goodnight to their guests as they retired. The general consensus was that everyone had enjoyed a great evening of delicious food, incredible wine, and dancing to a great local cover band called The Sultans of Swing. Deanna appeared in the foyer escorted by Gage and Andy, still wearing that supermodel bodysuit. She released her escorts and took Webber's hands in hers. "It was a perfect evening, Webber. I love you and wish you all the happiness you so obviously deserve."

"What, no snide remark?" Webber asked.

She gave him an evil look and moved over to Tristan. "And you," she said with a hint of mock jealously. "Even though you stole my man, I'm gonna be the bigger woman and wish you the best."

Tristan beamed and took her into his arms for a long embrace. "He ain't buying what you're selling, remember?" he whispered in her ear. "So it would have been a short, empty marriage."

She roared with laughter. "God, I love you," she said, giving him one final squeeze before releasing him. "This baby load is killing my back; I've got to get out of these heels."

Gage and Andy said their goodbyes and assured the boys they would see Deanna to her room.

Webber and Tristan were still standing in the foyer, gazing into one another's eyes when Cavan and Sam walked up and attempted to shoo them away. "Get out of here," Cavan urged. Sam handed them a bottle of champagne and two crystal flutes. "It's your honeymoon night. Go try and make some babies or something."

They all chuckled. "Thank you, guys, for everything," Tristan gushed.

"Yeah," Webber added. "Everything was absolutely perfect."

"You're welcome," Sam said, urging them to the door.

"Okay, okay," Tristan said, looking over his shoulder as they stepped outside. "We get the hint."

ON THE way to their room, Tristan popped the champagne and filled his and Webber's glasses. They strolled through the wedding garden, walking up the aisle then back down again, taking in all the simple beauty by the glow of the moonlight. "Everything was perfect, wasn't it?" Webber asked.

"In my opinion, I wouldn't have changed one perfect moment," Tristan agreed as he placed a slow gentle kiss on Webber's waiting lips.

Tristan slipped an arm around Webber's waist, and they walked up onto their deck, stopping at the railing and looking out over the pool area. "Webber, you know I'm dying to be with you right?"

Webber cocked an eyebrow. "Yeah…?" He hesitated.

"But I don't want to go in just yet."

"Any particular reason?"

"Once we go in, the evening is over, and I feel like I never want this night to end."

Webber covered Tristan's lips with his own. When the kiss ended, he brushed the hair out of Tristan's eyes. "Over our lifetime, I'm gonna give you a thousand nights just like this one."

"Then let's go," Tristan urged. "I have big plans, and they include seducing you." He stopped and raised his finger. "But so you'll know, all I really need is you. I'll make this memory last forever."

Webber felt warmed to his toes. "How about if we do this every five years?" he asked.

"That's a great idea," Tristan said, pushing Webber toward the door.

Webber felt his heart skip a beat with anticipation as he was backed across the deck to the door. After Tristan took the key out of his hand and slipped it into the lock, he stopped short and turned to Webber with a coy smile. "Shouldn't one of us be carrying the other over the threshold?"

"Do we flip a coin or something?" Webber teased, punching Tristan in the arm. "All these traditions."

"How about if we just step across the threshold arm in arm?" Tristan asked. "Will that work?"

"Don't see why not, although it would have been fun to carry you over."

"Why me?" Tristan barked with a chuckle. "I was thinking the same thing about you."

"Were you now?" Webber said with a tilt of his head.

"Uh huh," Tristan replied, smiling.

Webber took the champagne glass out of Tristan's hands and placed both glasses on the teak table next to the door. "Be careful what you ask for" was the last thing he said before he leaped into Tristan's arms and held on for dear life.

Tristan, although slightly smaller in height, was just as muscular, and he was obviously on his A game when he caught Webber with ease. But from the look on Tristan's face, Webber knew he'd achieved the element of surprise he'd gone for.

With a quirky grin, Tristan met Webber's eyes and pushed the door open with his foot, then turned to the side and carried him across the threshold, never breaking eye contact. Tristan put him down just inside the door and cupped the back of his neck, pulling him in for a long, sensual kiss. Releasing his neck but not breaking the kiss, Tristan slipped Webber's coat off over his shoulders and tossed it to the chair in the corner. The coat missed the chair completely and landed in a heap on the floor. Webber followed suit and did the same for Tristan, but he let the coat hit the floor without even bothering to toss it.

Still in the heat of the never-ending kiss, Webber worked his hands between them and loosened Tristan's tie, slipped the end through, and tossed it to the side. He fumbled with Tristan's buttons but eventually gave up and ripped the shirt open. He heard as much as felt a moan escape Tristan's mouth, and he was urged backward until he felt the bed at the back of his knees. In one push, Webber was flat on his back looking up at the man he loved. Tristan slowly unbuttoned the cuffs on what was left of his shirt, then pulled it off and tossed it aside. He kicked off his shoes and released his belt and pants, and Webber saw them fall to the floor.

He climbed on top of Webber and slowly removed his tie, then abruptly ripped Webber's shirt open without even trying to release the buttons. Webber felt goose bumps on his exposed skin as Tristan worked his way down. *God, this man is hot!*

Tristan released Webber's belt and pants but didn't remove them. He slid off the end of the bed, landing on the floor. Things were slower now, less frantic, more sensual. On his knees at Webber's feet, Tristan untied Webber's left shoe and slipped it off. He slowly and methodically massaged Webber's socked foot, hitting all the pressure points and causing involuntary moans of pleasure to leave Webber's lips. He slipped Webber's sock off and licked his foot from his heel to his toes. He kissed the tip of Webber's big toe and gently put his foot down. He removed the right shoe and repeated the procedure. When he was through, Tristan got to his feet and stood over Webber, reaching for his pants. Webber instinctively lifted his hips off of the bed, and Tristan slid the fabric down his muscular legs and over his feet to the floor.

Webber felt his erection growing steadily, quickly reaching the point of aching: aching to be touched, aching to be tasted, anything. As if he'd read Webber's mind, Tristan placed his mouth over Webber's length, nibbling lightly through his black cotton boxer briefs. He jerked from the sensation and fisted the sheets around him. Tristan continued to nibble tantalizing bites, slowly driving him crazy. Tristan peeled off

Webber's underwear and took him into his mouth, his warm wetness surrounding him, skin to skin, heat to heat. All Webber could do was thrash his head from side to side and moan in pleasure. Tristan reached up to Webber's chest and grabbed his nipples, twisting them between his thumbs and forefingers, never letting up his oral assault. Webber arched his back and hissed in delight with each movement Tristan made, longing for more, always more.

Tristan reached for the lubricant on the bedside table and coated Webber thoroughly. He moved his hands up and down making sure every inch of him was covered, nearly sending Webber over the top. Then Tristan turned his attention to himself. The sight of him applying lubrication and loosening himself for Webber was almost too much to handle. He closed his eyes and willed himself not to erupt as Tristan coated and worked both ends. When Tristan was well prepared, he climbed on top of Webber and straddled him. Tristan ran his fingers through Webber's hair and gripped his head in a firm hold as his their lips met in a fierce and frantic kiss. Tristan gyrated over him, surrounding his length with his tight, muscular glutes. He released Webber's head, eased up to his knees, never breaking the kiss, and positioned Webber at his opening. In one long, steady movement, Tristan's warmth surrounded him. Unrecognizable sounds escaped from deep within Webber as Tristan began to move up and down.

Tristan broke the kiss and sat upright, leaning back and riding Webber's rock hard erection. Webber reached up and stroked Tristan's length in time with Tristan's up and down movements. Webber couldn't remember seeing a more beautiful sight than the one in front of him right now. Tristan's head was thrown back, his eyes closed, and he was biting his bottom lip. His cheeks were flushed, and the look of sheer pleasure on his face warmed Webber beyond his wildest dreams. He was responsible for that look of pleasure on his husband's face, and he would spend every day for the rest of his life making sure he saw that look and gave Tristan the pleasure he so deserved.

A moan escaped Tristan's lips, bringing Webber back to the moment. He again focused his efforts on slow, gentle strokes that in turn coaxed jerks and pulses from deep within Tristan that squeezed him over and over.

"So good," Tristan whispered. "I won't last much longer."

"I'm there too," Webber admitted.

Tristan slid all the way down onto Webber and gyrated his hips, moaning in pleasure as Webber's erection massaged his prostate. He again started to move more frantically, with jerky but steady movements, quietly alerting Webber to his impending orgasm. Sensing Tristan was close to losing it, Webber matched Tristan's movements and speed.

Webber felt Tristan tighten around him as he moved frantically up and down. Tristan threw his head back as he lost control, spurts of warmth covering Webber's hand, chest, and stomach. As Tristan contracted around him, Webber's orgasm began to build from deep within, slowly working its way through his body. He released a low, guttural moan as he spilled deep inside of his husband. Webber rode the waves of pleasure as his orgasm shuddered through his body. He was still holding Tristan's fading erection as Tristan leaned up and kissed him deeply. He slipped from Tristan and immediately felt exposed. He missed Tristan's warmth surrounding and massaging him.

Tristan gave him one last peck before retreating to the bathroom. He came back with a warm, wet cloth and cleaned Webber and himself, then threw the cloth to the floor and climbed back in bed, snuggling against Webber and pulling the covers up around their necks.

"I love you," Webber said, kissing Tristan's temple. "That was incredible."

"It *was* pretty good, wasn't it?" Tristan teased. "I love you too, Mr. Moreau-Kincaid."

Those were the last words Webber heard before he drifted off into a peaceful slumber, thinking he had everything he'd ever wanted or needed lying in his arms.

THE next morning after breakfast, Tristan and Webber said good-bye to their guests one by one as everyone boarded the shuttle to the airport. They were taking off a little later with Kenton, Amani, and Kit, all of them heading back to Nectar Island for the honeymoon. Gage, Andy, and Deanna were the last in line to board the shuttle. After embracing

Webber, Gage took his big brother into his arms. "This has been an incredible experience. Be happy and always remember how proud I am of you. Love ya, big bro."

Tristan paused and fought back tears before he spoke. "Other than my new family, you and Andy are it. Please don't think less of me, but I won't reach out to the rest of our family again. I just can't."

Gage looked up at the bright blue sky. He took a deep breath and then nodded. "It's your decision and I won't interfere."

"Thank you for understanding, Gage."

Tristan hugged his brother and then Andy. He slapped Gage on the ass as he boarded the shuttle. "Say you'll at least think about joining us on Nectar Island in a couple weeks," Tristan said.

Gage stiffened at the gesture but looked over his shoulder with a slight smile. "Let me get Andy packed up and back on the road and I'll think about it."

Deanna hugged Webber. He kissed her then her belly. "Take care of our godchild," he said.

"We're both good," she said. "I'm so happy for you, Web. You deserve to be happy."

He took Tristan's hand. "I am happy and a lot of that is because of this man."

"Love you," she said, moving on to Tristan. "Don't let him give you any shit. He can get pretty bossy sometimes."

Tristan looked over at Webber and smiled. "I've handled him for the last two years. I'm sure I can handle him now."

"You just call me if you need a hand," she said, throwing her hands around his neck.

"I'll do that," he said, rubbing her belly. "Take care, honey, and call us every day and let us know how the baby's progressing."

Deanna smiled that big smile and stepped on the shuttle.

The doors closed and the shuttle drove off, Tristan and Webber waving goodbye until the shuttle disappeared around the curve in the road.

Webber wrapped Tristan up in his arms and gently kissed his temple. "We'll see them all again soon. Maybe we can drag Deanna and Gage to one of Andy's gigs. That would be fun, wouldn't it?"

Tristan nodded, his lip quivering a little, but didn't let go of Webber. "That would be fun, thanks."

An hour later, when they stepped out of the front door, the shuttle was back and Sam and Cavan were loading the luggage. Kenton, Amani, and Kit said their good-byes to Sam and Cavan and boarded the shuttle. Tristan and Webber turned around and looked at the inn again. "I just love this place," Webber said.

"Me too," Tristan agreed.

Cavan and Sam walked up and stood next to them. "Not that we were eavesdropping or anything, but we heard what you said. Sam and I love this place too, but we think we're about done with it."

Webber and Tristan looked at each other. "Really?" Webber asked, breaking eye contact with Tristan and turning to Cavan. "You're going to sell?"

"I'm afraid so," Sam said. "It's time. We've been at it for almost ten years and we think we might want to do something else."

"Please promise you won't do anything until you talk to us," Webber insisted.

"Seriously?" Cavan asked. "Would you consider buying this place?"

"Hell yeah," Webber said, smiling at Tristan. "Give us a little time to discuss it and we'll call next week."

Cavan smiled. "All righty then," he said, offering his hand to Webber for a shake.

Webber accepted his hand then pulled him in for a hug. "Thanks for everything. It was perfect."

"We're so glad you're happy. We feel a lot of pressure with weddings because we only get one chance to get it right."

"Well, you got this one right," Tristan assured them. "We'll be in touch."

Eight

NECTAR ISLAND was as beautiful as Tristan remembered. They'd been there for close to two months already, and he couldn't believe how time was flying by. They spent most of their days by the pool or on one of the boats cruising the azure waters of the Caribbean. They island hopped regularly, frequenting Foxy's, Willie T's, the Soggy Dollar Bar, and the Virgin Gorda baths. In the evenings, they watched magnificent sunsets, ate incredible meals prepared by Amani, then made love most of the night, starting it all over again the next day.

Gage had come for a week as he'd promised, and since Deanna could no longer travel, she called every day or so to update them on her pregnancy. They were extremely happy and had no real plans to leave. They knew that eventually they would get back to Atlanta, but they'd been in serious discussions with Cavan and Sam to buy the inn. The only dilemma was, would they keep it as a business and get someone to run it, or would they convert it to a private residence? They had an architect drawing up plans for converting the Guest House back to a barn and the Carriage House into an actual guesthouse.

TRISTAN and Webber were lying by the pool sipping some tropical concoction Kenton had whipped up when Webber's cellphone rang. He looked at the caller ID. "It's Deanna."

He touched the screen, accepting the call. "Hey, D. How's little Webber?"

"He wants out," she said with a little panic in her voice.

"What?" Webber said excitedly. "Are you in labor?"

"I'm afraid so," she replied. "It just started, and I'm on the way to the hospital."

Tristan was staring at him with eyes as big as saucers. Webber reached out and touched him on the arm. "We'll be there as soon as we can," Webber assured her. "Just stay calm until we get there, then you can have a nervous breakdown. And don't have that baby without us."

Deanna chuckled. "I'll shove a cork up there and strap my knees together. Just please hurry! I hate to admit it, Webber, but I'm a little scared."

"It'll be okay, D. Just hang in there. We're on our way," Webber said as he disconnected the call.

Tristan was already up and dialing his cell phone. "I'll make travel arrangements. You start packing."

"I'm on it," Webber replied, hopping out of his chair and heading for the house.

An hour later, Tristan and Webber were waving goodbye to Kenton and Amani from the helicopter as they took off for St. Thomas to board their private jet to Los Angeles.

Their sedan pulled up in front of Cedars-Sinai Hospital, and almost before it came to a complete stop, Tristan and Webber were out and heading for the front door, their duffle bags slung over their shoulders. They had talked to Deanna a few times once they'd landed and knew she had a birthing suite in the Labor and Delivery Unit on the third floor. They rode the elevator up and stopped at the nurse's station to get further directions. Minutes later they were opening the door. Deanna was sitting in a chair with an IV attached to her arm watching some entertainment news show that was reporting she'd been admitted to the hospital, about to give birth. She looked up as they walked in. "How do they know these things so fast?" she said in amazement.

Webber chuckled as he stooped down at her chair. "How're you doing, kiddo?"

"You mean besides feeling like I need to pass a basketball?"

"I guess so, yeah," Webber responded.

"Oh, I'm okay, I guess. The labor pains are getting steadier and closer together, but I've been holding off on an epidural until they get unbearable."

"Take the drugs," Tristan encouraged, stooping down next to Webber.

"My God," she said. "Look at your tans. You look great."

"We have gotten a lot of sun, haven't we?"

"You look like a Coppertone commercial."

Deanna squeezed the side of the chair. "Here we go again."

She tensed up, closed her eyes, and bit her bottom lip, pushing through the labor pain.

She opened her eyes and exhaled, smiling slightly.

"How bad are they?" Tristan asked.

"Manageable right now. The doctor just left and I'm dilated about six centimeters, but the contractions aren't consistent. There were coming every six minutes, then five, then back up to eight minutes."

"Is that any indication that something is wrong?" Webber asked.

"The doctor said no, but to just give it a couple more hours," she said with a pout. "Two more damn hours."

"Well, if it's any consolation, you look great," Webber said.

"Thanks," she whined with a smirk.

Webber and Tristan pulled up a couple of chairs and sat with her. For the next two and a half hours, they each held her hands while she pushed through each contraction. They seemed a little more intense with each one, but the timing was still inconsistent.

Tristan and Webber stepped out of the suite when the doctor came in to check her progress. When he was finished with his examination, he invited them back in.

"It looks like she's dilated about seven centimeters," he explained. "But we need to get the contractions a little more consistent. I suggest you take turns walking her around the hall. Nine times out of ten, that will do the trick."

Tristan volunteered to take the first watch while Webber ran downstairs to grab a cup of coffee. He and Deanna walked up and down the halls, Deanna pushing her IV pole with one hand and holding on to Tristan with the other.

"I swear, if the paparazzi gets up here and takes a picture of me like this, I'll sue their damn pants off," she joked.

Tristan looked at her and smiled. "Webber's right. You look great, so don't give that another thought."

When they made it back to the room, Webber was ready to take over, offering Tristan a hot cup of coffee in exchange for a hot supermodel, albeit a pregnant one.

"Very funny," she said when he made the offer. "Keep that shit up and I'll show you just how hard a hot, pregnant supermodel can kick a man in the groin."

"Point taken," Webber said with a squeamish look on his face.

Tristan did the handoff and accepted the hot coffee. "See you guys in a few. Keep up the good work, D," he added.

Webber and Deanna started down the hall. Tristan watched until they turned the corner, then headed to the bathroom.

WHILE they walked up and down the halls, lap after lap, corridor after corridor, Webber filled Deanna in on everything he and Tristan had done on their honeymoon. He talked endlessly, anything to keep her mind off of the obvious. They'd just made the third lap when she stopped dead in her tracks and gripped Webber's hand extremely hard. Their eyes met and Webber instantly knew something was wrong. A stricken look of horror contorted Deanna's delicate features, seconds before the color drained from her face. "Webber!" was all she said.

He heard a noise like someone spilling a bucket of water on the floor and looked down to see bright red blood everywhere. They were surrounded with seemingly gallons of blood. Deanna went limp next to him, and he barely caught her in time, easing her down to the floor. "Deanna!" He screamed. "D!" His heart was racing and panic filled every fiber of his being. *Oh God, help us!*

He tried to get to his feet, but he kept slipping in the blood and falling back to the floor. "Deanna!" he screamed. "Someone help us! Please! Help!"

Deanna was unconscious and not responding. Webber instinctively looked around for the one person he always knew he could count on. "Tristan," he screamed. "Help me!"

It seemed like forever, but it was only seconds before he saw Tristan round the corner followed by medical personnel. They had Deanna up and on a stretcher, taking vitals and yelling all these medical terms Webber didn't understand. Suddenly a nurse screamed, "Call a code blue," as more medical personnel surrounded Deanna. Before he could wrap his mind around what was happening or had a chance to ask, they were racing down the hall pushing the stretcher at breakneck speed. Webber could only watch in horror as they wheeled her through double doors at the end of the hall until the doors closed and he lost sight of them.

As if in slow motion, Webber looked down at his blood-soaked clothes. The next thing he knew, Tristan was leading him somewhere, but he was in a fog, following without conscious thought. Tristan's mouth was moving as if he was talking to him, but Webber couldn't make out what he was saying. It was a backdrop of jumbled noise to the image of Deanna's face right before she collapsed.

Webber vaguely heard one of the nurses tell Tristan she would come to the suite as soon as she knew anything. Tristan was asking her something about a shower, needing to get Webber cleaned up, but it made no sense. She asked if he needed something to wear, but Tristan assured her that he had some clothing with them.

He felt himself being led down the hall, and then they were in the bathroom of Deanna's suite. Tristan stripped him and put him in the shower. He stood under the hot water and stared at the blood running down the drain. His knees started to shake, and the tremors worked their way up until his entire body was trembling uncontrollably. He felt Tristan's strong arms supporting him, encircling him, whispering words of encouragement. The combination of the hot water and the sound of Tristan's voice soothed him and the shaking started to subside. Tristan washed the blood off him, led him out of the shower, and sat him down on the closed toilet seat.

"Web, please talk to me. You're starting to scare me."

Webber looked at him with an empty stare. "The blood. There was so much blood."

"I know Web, I know. But the doctors have her now. She'll be alright."

"They called a code blue," Webber mumbled. "A code blue. That means her heart stopped. Oh God, Tris, a code blue."

Tristan cupped Webber's face in both his hands, forcing him to meet his gaze. "Hey, stop that. We have to believe they will take care of her, okay?"

Webber still felt the dread surging through him, but Tristan's warm hands against his cheeks grounded him and he nodded.

"Let's get dressed so we'll be ready when they come in to talk to us."

Webber didn't argue and did as he was told. He watched as Tristan rummaged through his bag and pulled out underwear and socks, a pair of blue jeans, and a turtleneck. Webber took the clothes and quietly dressed, then sat in a chair staring straight ahead.

Tristan then pulled clothes out of his bag, dressed, took a seat next to Webber, and held his hand. "Tell me what you're feeling."

Webber didn't speak but squeezed his hand, letting Tristan know that he'd heard him and understood.

Before Tristan could ask anything else, the door opened and Deanna's doctor stood in the doorway. Webber jumped to his feet, but froze in place. He felt Tristan standing next to him and holding his hand. The doctor looked back and forth between them with a grave expression. He removed his surgical cap and ran his fingers through his hair. "I'm very sorry. We did everything we could."

His brain was obviously still functioning in slow motion. No way did he just hear what he thought he did. It was incomprehensible. "I'm sorry. I must have heard you wrong." He looked at the doctor for more clarification, but the grim look on his face as he shook his head, said it all.

He sat back down in his chair; more like collapsed and put his head between his legs. Tristan was on the floor at his feet, rubbing the back of his head. The doctor continued to talk. "Ms. Lynn experienced something called abruptio placentae. This occurs when the placenta, the organ that nourishes the fetus, separates from the wall of the uterus, causing the mother to hemorrhage."

"Meaning?" Tristan asked, his voice low.

"It means she began to bleed uncontrollably. We had a small window of time to control the bleeding, about three minutes. We did everything we could. "

"The baby?" Tristan asked.

"She's in the Neonatal Intensive Care Unit and they're running some tests."

"She?" Tristan whispered.

"Yes, it's a girl," The doctor explained. "But we don't know how long she was deprived of oxygen and if she'll have any long term affects. The fact that this happened in the hospital gave us the very few minutes we needed to save her. Unfortunately, there was no way to save Ms. Lynn. I'm very sorry."

Webber was hearing all of this, but it just wasn't registering. *Deanna can't be gone, she just can't. Any minute I'm going to wake up. This has to be a nightmare.*

"I'll let you know when you can see the baby," the doctor said. "Again, I'm very sorry."

"Stop saying you're sorry!" Webber screamed. "This is all an ugly dream. I just need to wake up. Tristan, please wake me up. I need to talk to Deanna. I need to make sure she's okay."

I'm sorry, we did everything we could. I'm sorry, I'm sorry, I'm sorry! Abruptio placentae. Bled out. Hemorrhage. No! Webber grabbed both sides of his head and squeezed.

"Tristan, make it go away. Please take me to see Deanna."

He vaguely heard Tristan talking to him, but he felt like he was spiraling out of control. He'd never been so scared, so hopeless.

"Web, look at me, please," Tristan pleaded.

Webber tried to focus on Tristan's soothing voice, tried to come back to reality. It took every bit of strength to complete the simple task of raising his head, but he did it. When he met Tristan's gaze, tears were streaming down his cheeks. "Deanna's gone. Baby, I'm so sorry. But I'm here for you. Talk to me."

"No, she's not gone," he said in a defiant tone. "This is all a horrible nightmare."

"I wish it were, baby," Tristan whispered. He pulled Webber into his arms. "Tell me what I can do."

Webber stood up and pushed him away. Tristan fought to try to keep his balance, but he was unsuccessful and landed on his ass in the middle of the hospital suite. Webber paced back and forth. "She can't be gone, she can't be gone, she can't be gone," he mumbled over and over.

Webber stopped pacing and looked at Tristan, still on the floor where he'd pushed him away. And suddenly the reality of the last hour came crashing down on him. *Oh my God, she is gone.* His legs gave out from under him and he fell to his knees, covering his face with both hands. "She's gone. Deanna's dead," he sobbed. "She's really dead."

Tristan got to his knees and crawled over to Webber, wrapping him up in his arms and rocking him back and forth. "I know. Baby, I loved her too. Just let it all out."

They stayed there on the floor in the middle of the hospital suite and cried together until they were cried out. A nurse came in once, but stepped out when her eyes met Tristan's and he nodded, indicating that they were okay but needed more time.

Webber felt secure wrapped in Tristan's arms. His face was up against Tristan's chest with Tristan's cheek resting on the top of his head. When the tears stopped flowing, Webber pushed himself away and got to his feet. He offered a hand to Tristan and they stood gazing into each other's eyes. He recognized the concerned look on Tristan's face and wanted to ease it of some pain. "I'll be okay," he whispered. "Thank you."

He wanted to wash his face so he headed for the bathroom. "No!" he heard Tristan yell, but it was too late. He felt like a bullet had pierced his chest when he saw the pile of bloody clothes on the bathroom floor. He stumbled back and hit the doorframe, grabbing for anything to keep him from ending up on the floor again.

In a flash, Tristan was at his side, steadying him. "It's okay. Web, I got this. You go and sit down. I'll get a warm cloth and be right back."

Webber did as he was told, and moments later, Tristan appeared in the doorway, closing the bathroom door behind him.

Webber rubbed the warm cloth over his face and held it there, just wishing he and Tristan were back in the Caribbean basking in the warm sunshine. Anywhere but in this living hell of a hospital room.

The nurse came in again and smiled weakly at them. "The doctor said you can see the baby now."

"Oh my God, the baby," Webber mumbled almost to himself. "A girl. Deanna's baby girl."

Tristan nodded, taking Webber by the hand and following the nurse to the NIC unit. When they reached the glass-enclosed room, the doctor was still examining the tiny baby.

"She's not as little as I thought she was going to be," Tristan said. "Web, she's beautiful."

Webber couldn't speak. He simply starred at the little rosy-cheeked baby girl lying in an incubator with a label that said "Baby Lynn."

The enormous loss hit him again, and he stepped away from the glass, not wanting to look at the infant. Webber watched from the corner as the doctor came out and started speaking to Tristan. He wanted to hear what they were saying, but he couldn't bear to look at the baby, not now, maybe not ever.

When Tristan and the doctor finished talking, the doctor went back into the NIC unit and Tristan came over to him. "The doctor says all indications are that the baby will be fine. They'll need to run more tests over the next month, but if all goes well, we can take her home in thirty days."

"Take her home?" Webber mumbled.

"Web, she's our responsibility. We promised Deanna we would raise the baby if anything happened to her, remember?"

Webber's knees became weak again and he felt a panic attack coming on. Tristan must have seen the look on his face and took him by the arm. "It's okay. Web, we can talk about this later. I need to get you to a hotel."

"I can't leave her here alone," Webber whispered.

"She's got plenty of people taking care of her, Web. She'll be fine."

"Not the baby!" Webber spit out. "Deanna."

"Web," Tristan said softly. "Deanna's gone. Her body's here, but her spirit has moved on. There's nothing more we can do for her now."

Webber knew Tristan was right, but he didn't think he could leave her here alone. Then his knees began to buckle as a thought occurred to him. He grabbed on to Tristan to steady himself. "Oh God, Tris, I need to call her father," he said, fighting a wave of nausea. "I don't want this getting out before I talk to her father."

Webber dug his cellphone out of his pocket and walked farther down the corridor. The weight of what he was about to do stabbed at his heart. He held the phone to his ear with one hand and rubbed the back of his neck with the other. He ran his fingers through his hair over and over and then pressed his palm to his stomach, still trying to fight the nausea that was getting worse with each breath. When Deanna's father answered the phone, Webber's voice cracked. His mouth moved but nothing came out. *Man up, Kincaid. You've got to do this. Speak damn it.* "Ah, Mr. Lynn, this is Webber Kincaid. I'm afraid I have some bad news."

When Webber was through giving Deanna's father the worst news a parent could ever expect to hear, he ended the call. He dropped his head and his tears flowed. Tristan walked over and wrapped Webber in his arms and rubbed his back, holding his lover as they sobbed together.

THE first week after Deanna's death had flown by. Webber kept himself very busy planning the funeral, and Tristan had spent most of his time at the hospital, continually telling Webber it was important that they forge a bond with the baby early on. But Webber had used the funeral as an excuse to avoid the hospital and the baby, knowing it was wrong, but trying to deal with the unresolved feelings of resentment where the baby was concerned.

It was obvious to Webber that Tristan knew he was having trouble dealing with losing Deanna and the issues surrounding the new little person in their family, but each time Tristan had tried to bring it up, Webber had avoided the topic at all costs. He felt bad enough about how he was avoiding the baby, but he wasn't ready to talk about it or deal with the reality of it all.

There was no way to describe Deanna's funeral other than intimate, understated and elegant. Webber had followed every one of her instructions down to the letter. The Cathedral of Our Lady of the Angels was full of an abundance of her favorite flowers, specially chosen music, and a hand-selected list of family and close friends in attendance. The short service ended at the Forest Lawn Memorial Park, where she was laid to rest in a gorgeous bronze and gold casket covered in rows and rows of foxglove and ivy.

After the service, Tristan had insisted they stop by the hospital, but thankfully, he hadn't forced him to interact with the baby. He watched from the back of the NIC unit as Tristan fed the little bundle in his arms and talked to her in soft, soothing tones. His heart was caught between so much love and so much loss. The baby was part of her. He knew somewhere in his heart there was love for her, but she was also the reason Deanna was no longer with him. He knew logically he was being selfish and stupid, but the loss and the pain were all too new to sort through.

Tristan looked over his shoulder. "Webber, we need to give her a name," he whispered. "It's time."

Webber couldn't quite find anything to say, so he didn't respond.

Tristan continued to talk to the baby is a soft voice. "I think we should name you after your mother," he said. "Webber, what do you think of Deanna Lynn Moreau-Kincaid?"

Webber felt a lump form in his throat. His heart started beating very fast and his bottom lips started to quiver. He stepped out of the NIC unit without a word, not wanting to lose his composure in front of the nurses. He stopped just outside the door and leaned against the wall to steady himself. He rested his head back and closed his eyes. "Deanna Lynn Moreau-Kincaid."

Tears started rolling down his cheeks, and he felt a finger lightly brushing them away. He opened his eyes to see Tristan standing in front of him with so much love in his eyes he could hardly stand it. He threw his arms around Tristan's shoulders and buried his face in Tristan's neck. He didn't move, he didn't talk, he just held on until he felt strong enough to break the connection.

Tristan stroked his face with the backs of his fingers. "It's going to be alright, Web, it really is," he reassured him. "Stop beating yourself up for not accepting the baby right now. You're still grieving. I get it and I'll love her enough for both of us right now."

Webber felt a flood of relief at the few simple words. Tristan was giving him the time he needed to sort through his emotions and wasn't judging him. He threw his arms around Tristan again. "I love you so much."

"I love you too, Webber. We'll get through this together, and on the other side, we'll be a family," he promised. "You, me, and little D."

BY THE end of the next week, the doctor told Tristan that little Deanna had passed all her tests with flying colors and although her progress would need to be monitored very closely, she was ready to go home. Wanting little D to have a strong connection to her mother, they'd had everything Deanna bought for her shipped to Atlanta. Tristan had been communicating with Sophie on a daily basis, so he'd known everything had arrived and little D's room was ready and waiting. Webber was named the executor of Deanna's will, so he'd spent a good bit of time getting her affairs in order. Besides a few personal things she'd left to her father, everything else went to the baby, including the proceeds from the sale of her Bellaire home. Webber painstakingly emptied the house, saved anything he thought little D might want when she was grown, donated the rest to charity, and listed the house with a real estate broker.

The last couple of days, he accompanied Tristan to the hospital but still wasn't holding the baby and interacting with her at all. Baby steps, Tristan kept telling himself.

The next morning they checked out of the hotel, picked up the baby at the hospital, and boarded the private jet back to Atlanta. When they pulled into the driveway, Sophie was there to meet them. She took the baby out of Tristan's arms and held her close to her bosom.

"She's beautiful, just like her mama," Sophie cooed. "It's going to be so much fun having a little one around the house again."

Tristan smiled. "You take her in and I'll help Webber with the luggage."

Sophie beamed and turned toward the house with the little one in her arms.

Webber was taking the bags from the driver. Tristan put his hands on Webber's back. "Are you okay, Web?"

"I guess so," Webber confessed. "It all seems so surreal to me right now. I really don't know how to feel."

"Feel the way you feel," Tristan suggested. "I know you, Webber. You have more love in your heart than anyone I know. You'll get through this. We'll get through this."

They carried all the bags in and dropped them in the foyer. Tristan kissed Webber on the cheek. "I'm gonna check on Sophie and the baby. See how little D likes her new room."

Webber nodded. "I'm gonna check e-mail and do a little research on Deanna's holdings and investments. I want to make sure she'd invested wisely."

Tristan bounced off toward the nursery, and Webber disappeared into his study and took a seat behind his desk. A couple of hours later, immersed up to his neck in financials, he heard Tristan's voice coming his way. "Sophie, the baby monitor's on the foyer table," he yelled.

"I'll be right there," Sophie yelled from the kitchen.

Tristan stepped into Webber's study. "How's it going in here?"

"It's going," Webber replied. "She's done really well for herself. She invested wisely."

"Good to hear it. She was one smart cookie."

"That she was," Webber agreed. "Are you running out?"

"Not for long," Tristan promised. "I need to pick up a few baby things, but don't worry. D's been fed and is napping and Sophie has the baby monitor."

He walked around the desk, dropping into Webber's lap. "I'll be right back," he said, kissing him on the cheek.

"Be careful and hurry back," Webber said. "I love you."

"Love you too. Don't work too hard."

Webber was again buried in financials, trying to make heads or tails of some real estate deal Deanna had invested in, when he heard the baby crying. He tried to focus on what he was doing, but the crying got louder and louder. "Sophie!" he yelled through his study door.

No answer.

He got up from his desk and walked into the foyer, and the baby monitor was still on the entry table. "Sophie!" He yelled again and waited. Still no answer.

He picked up the baby monitor and headed to the kitchen. Sophie was nowhere to be found, and the baby's cries were sounding more frantic. "Where in the hell is Sophie? And Tristan should be back by now. It's been over an hour. Damn it."

He hesitated, then walked toward the nursery, then stopped. He turned back around and called for Sophie again. "Damn," he cursed when she still didn't answer.

He paced back and forth, the baby monitor in his hand revealing a very angry baby on the other end.

"The hell with it," he mumbled.

He walked to the nursery and stuck his head in the little pink and yellow room. He stepped up to the crib and looked down at the screaming baby. Her face was beet red and her eyes were wet.

"Shhhhh," he said gently patting her stomach. "Your daddy will be back real soon."

That didn't work. He walked to the hall and stuck his head out, calling for Sophie again. When he heard no response, he went back to the crib. He put the baby monitor down and hesitantly slipped his hands under the baby and lifted her to his chest.

Her wails seemed to subside a little, but she was still screaming bloody murder.

"Shhhhh, what's wrong, little one?" he said in a hushed tone. "It's alright. You're safe."

He sat down in the rocking chair and started to move slowly back and forth. Her crying slowed to more of a hiccupping sound, and she opened her blue eyes, looking up at him. "That's better," he whispered.

He studied the baby for the first time and saw that she really was beautiful. Her baby-fine blonde hair glistened and her deep blue eyes sparkled. The little cleft in her chin was adorable, and he melted when he noticed that her little fingers were wrapped tightly around his thumb. When she starred up at him, he saw Deanna in all of her features. "You sure look a lot like your mommy, you know that?"

The crying had now turned into cooing, and he thought she was actually flirting with him.

"You not only look like your mommy, you flirt just like her as well."

She seemed like she was wiggling a bit, like maybe she had a gas bubble or something. He thought a second and then remembered something about putting her over his shoulder and patting her back. Burping, that was it. He lifted her little body, careful to support her head, and gently patted her back. She smelled divine, all soft and sweet and innocent. A few minutes later a little hiccup came out of her tiny mouth, and he had to smile to himself. *Mission accomplished.*

He gently cradled her in his arms again, and she immediately closed her eyes and went right back to sleep as he gently rocked her.

TRISTAN came in the front door, arms loaded with packages, and looked into Webber's study, but it was empty. He dropped the packages and went to the kitchen. Sophie was prepping for dinner. "Hey," he said. "Have you seen Webber?"

"No honey. I went down to the wine cellar for a few minutes, but last I saw him, he was tucked away in his study."

"Is Deanna okay?"

"Not a peep out of her," Sophie said.

Tristan looked around the kitchen but didn't see the baby monitor. "I'll take the monitor with me. Where is it?"

Sophie froze. "Oh Tristan, I'm so sorry. Stupid me. It must still be on the foyer table."

Tristan walked back to the foyer, but the monitor wasn't there. His heart dropped to his stomach, and he ran to the nursery with Sophie on his heels. When he rounded the door, he stopped dead in his tracks. Little D was in Webber's strong arms, and he was rocking her back and forth, singing to her softly. He took Sophie by the arm and squeezed. *Everything's going to be okay!*

Sophie smiled and slowly turned away, apparently giving them the privacy she thought they needed. Tristan's heart was full as he quietly walked into the room, laying his hand on Webber's shoulder. Webber stopped singing and looked up, smiling. His eyes were soaked, but they seemed to be happy tears. "She's beautiful," he whispered.

"She is," Tristan agreed. "And her daddies are going to give her the best life ever."

Don't miss the beginning of the story in

SCOTTY CADE left Corporate America and twenty-five years of marketing and public relations behind to buy an inn & restaurant on the island of Martha's Vineyard with his partner of fourteen years.

He started writing stories as soon as he could read, but only recently for publication. When not at the inn, you can find him on the bow of his boat writing m/m romance novels with his Shetland sheepdog Mavis at his side. Being from the South and a lover of commitment and fidelity, most of his characters find their way to long, healthy relationships, however long it takes them to get there. He believes that, in the end, the boy should always get the boy.

Scotty and his partner are avid boaters and live aboard their boat, spending the summers on Martha's Vineyard and winters in Charleston, SC, and Savannah, GA.

Visit Scotty at http://www.scottycade.com and Scotty Cade on Facebook and Twitter. You can contact him at scotty@scottycade.com.

Also from SCOTTY CADE

Foundation *of* Love

SCOTTY CADE
AND Z.B. MARSHALL

http://www.dreamspinnerpress.com

Also from SCOTTY CADE

http://www.dreamspinnerpress.com

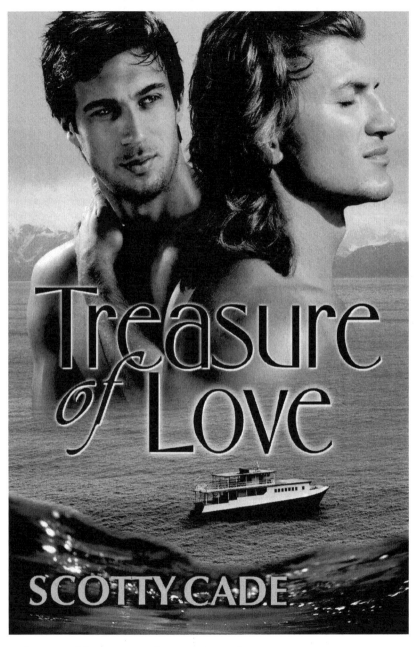

Made in the USA
Coppell, TX
29 October 2021